Forbidden
A Love to Die For

A NOVEL BY

MYIESHA MASON

JOIN IT'S MAJOR

To submit a manuscript for our review, email us at
submissions@majorkeypublishing.com

PROLOGUE

LUVLEIGH

"**O**h my god, RJ, you're so darn stupid," I yelled at Romeo Jr. as I wiped the water out my face. He purposely did a cannonball near us girls, splashing us with water.

"Shut up," he said, coming up from under the water. "You know you like when I splash you," he whispered into my ear as he brushed up against my butt before swimming away. I looked over at my cousin Ladi, and best friend, Hunter as they both witnessed the interaction between RJ and me.

"Yeah, you know you like it when he splashes you," they both joked, before giggling in unison.

"Y'all can shut up, too," I said, splashing them with water as they both started splashing me back.

I was fourteen-years-old and the youngest child of Xavier and Juliet Carter. I had two older twin brothers, Star and Sun, who were sixteen-years-old and annoying as hell. With them two, plus my daddy, I felt like I had three fathers. The three of them were overprotective of me, which got on my last nerve. It wasn't much I could get into while always being under their watchful eyes, or under the watch of my father's bodyguards. I couldn't go anywhere without them. I swear I couldn't wait to go off to college in four years.

My mother, on the other hand, barely paid attention to me at times. There were times when I thought that she didn't like me as much. I thought it was because of how much attention my daddy paid me and how I technically got away with everything. My mother was a little controlling. She controlled everything my brothers did, like what they wore and ate. She did that shit with my daddy too, but with my father, I think he just did what she wanted out of love. With me though, that shit wasn't going down. She tried to tell me what to do all the time, but I would ignore her and do what I wanted. She knew as long as my daddy was around, I was going to show my ass.

My father was a pretty powerful guy in the music industry. He and his partner, Romeo, owned one of the most lucrative record labels on the east coast, and soon the entire United States. DYMND records had the best musical talent signed to the label.

My dad was rich and famous, and there were always people out there who would do anything to be the next rising star; and I do mean anything. I've had someone pretend to be a substitute teacher just to hand me one of their demos to give to my father. Since that day, my father assigned me a damn bodyguard to sit in the hallways of my school, while I sat in class and learned.

My dad's partner and best friend Romeo, who I called Uncle Rome, was RJ's father. RJ and I were raised as cousins, but we knew we weren't blood cousins, so it didn't stop the physical, nor sexual attraction we felt for one another at our young age. Whenever people weren't around, we flirted with one another, but that was the furthest we've ever gone. RJ was seventeen and the oldest son of Uncle Rome. Uncle Rome also had two other kids, Leo and Aries, who were fifteen-years-old. They weren't as annoying as RJ though. They just sat and played video games all day, like now. They were sitting in the grass with their PSPs, probably battling each other in Pokémon or some-thing. Then it was their cousin, Fatima, who wanted to be called Fa. If you asked me, I thought she was going to be a bulldagger. She dressed like a boy, and she didn't have any girlfriends. My Uncle Rome would bring her over to hang with Hunter, Ladi, and I a few times, but she would always end up hanging in the basement with Star and Sun. Ladi and Hunter never liked when she was around anyway, because she would just sit there and quietly stare at us.

"I'll be back. I'm going to go take a shower before cheerleading practice," I told my girls as I climbed out of the pool. I grabbed my hot pink beach towel and wrapped it around my body as I walked into our seven-bedroom mansion in Ramsey, New Jersey.

I hated that I had to leave the barbeque, but if I wanted to make captain, it was a must that I show up to every practice on time to show my coach that I was dedicated to the team.

When I got into my bedroom, I quickly grabbed all my toiletries out my bathroom and brought them to the hallway bathroom because my bathroom was being remodeled.

I removed my bathing suit and stepped into the shower, sliding the shower door shut behind me. I didn't want to be in here for too long because this was the bathroom designated for our guest to use.

I was under the water rinsing the shampoo from my hair when I heard the bathroom door open. I thought I had locked the door, but I guess didn't.

"I'm in here!" I shouted.

"So," he replied. I recognized the voice as Romeo Jr.'s. I slightly slid the shower door open to look at him.

"So get the fuck out, damn," I told him, sliding the door back as I continued to wash my body. I heard piss hitting the water inside of the toilet bowl. Without thinking, I slid the shower door back open, ready to curse him out, but once I opened the door it was like my eyes were glued to his penis. I couldn't stop looking at it.

"If you wanted to see my dick, all you had to do was ask," he said, looking at me with a creepy ass smile on his face.

"Boy, nobody wanna see your little ugly ding-a-ling."

"So why you still looking at it?"

"Because, I can't believe how little it is," I lied, shutting the shower door back. It was nothing little about that thing, but I wasn't going to let him know. He was already too conceited. Although I was a virgin, I've seen penises before, but none as big as his.

"You better get used to it, you're going to be married to it one day."

I rolled my eyes. He was always saying when we got older that we were going to be married, but I ignored him every time. I went back to washing before the shower door suddenly opened. "Now that you see mine, can I see yours?" he asked.

"You wanna see my dick?" I asked him, not caring that I was standing in front of him naked. "You gay?"

"Do I look gay?"

"With those big, pink, wet lips, and that curly hair, yes; you look a little suspect."

"The girls love these lips," he said, giving me a little LL lip-licking action. I jerked my head back and then placed the palm of my hand in the middle of his face, mushing him before shutting the shower door back. I laughed, shook my head, and went back to washing.

The shower door came open again and this time, he was standing there without his swimming trunks. He stepped into the shower with me.

"What do you think you are doing?" I asked.

"I have football practice, I need to shower too."

"Then go in another shower. I just washed and you're getting your dirt on me," I complained.

"I don't want to get in the other showers."

"Why not?'

"Because you won't be in there to wash my back. Here," he said handing me the bar soap. I looked at him like he had just lost his mind. He opened my hand and he placed the soap inside the palm of my hand, closed it, and then turned around. I rolled my eyes and hung up my loofah before washing his back.

"Here, I'm done now get out," I told him. He turned around and started washing the suds off his back. My eyes had once again dropped down to his penis, which was standing up and close to poking me in the belly button.

"You know, if you weren't enjoying me being in here, you could have got out a long time ago," he said.

I looked up and into his smiling face.

"You are so right."

I was about to step out of the shower when he pulled me back, pinning me against the wall and kissed me. I didn't fight back, I just stood there and kissed him back. As we were kissing, he grabbed my hand and placed it onto his hard, but smooth penis.

I mimicked him by grabbing his hand and placing it between my legs, and he began to make circular motions with his fingers. We stopped kissing and just stood there, touching one another.

There was a knock on the bathroom door which caused me to jump and I released him, but he never released me. "The door is locked," he whispered.

"One minute," I shouted.

"Take your time, baby girl," my Uncle Rome's voice spoke. I stood there with my mouth open while RJ just stood there smiling like we weren't about to get caught. He grabbed my hand and placed it back onto his penis, but I removed it.

"Your father is right outside."

"So," he said.

"What do you mean so? What are we going to do?" I whispered.

"Don't worry, baby girl, I'll go use your parents," my uncle spoke once again.

"See, he's gone."

"Yeah, and so am I," I said, jumping out of the shower. I grabbed my towel and wrapped it around my body. RJ shut the water off, climbed out, and wrapped himself in a towel as well. He pressed me up against the door and started to kiss me again. I had to admit that I was really enjoying the way his lips felt.

"How about we continue this in your room?" he suggested.

"No, I have cheerleading practice in like an hour," I replied.

"It ain't gon' take long," he said, kissing me again. Although I wanted to say no, it was like his lips had a power over my mind, causing me to say *ok.*

I opened the bathroom door and looked down both ways of the hallway before we quickly darted across the hallway to my room.

When we got inside, I shut the door and made sure to lock it. By the time I turned around, RJ already had his towel dropped down to the floor and was walking up to me.

He removed my towel and swept me off my feet before carrying me over to the bed. He laid me down as he hovered over top of me. I couldn't believe that I was about to do this.

"I'm a virgin, so don't hurt me," I warned him.

"I'll try not to," he responded.

"And make sure you pull-out, I'm not trying to be a teen mom."

"Shut up, Luvleigh. I know what I'm doing," he said, as he slowly started to slide into me. I tried to scream out in pain, but he muffled it by placing his hands over my mouth. "It'll start feeling better soon," he whispered into my ear. "Just relax, baby."

I tried doing as he told me, but it was still hurting. When he said soon, I was expecting soon to be sooner than what it was.

After about a minute, I started to get in the groove of it and began opening my legs wider, pulling him into me deeper.

It was really starting to feel good. That was until he pulled his penis out of me and released his sperm all over my satin lavender comforter. *Damn that's going to stain*, was all I thought.

After he caught his breath, he stood up and walked into my bathroom. The sink was still functioning, so he grabbed two washcloths, wet them, and came back into the bedroom and handed me one.

He cleaned himself off and I cleaned myself off. I noticed the little remnants of blood on the washcloth, but I had read that was normal during the first time. I stood up and went to get dressed into my practice uniform.

"You know, this doesn't mean we're like boyfriend and girlfriend, right," RJ said. I turned and looked at him with the *ewww* face.

"Eww, that's disgusting. You're like my cousin," I said, making him laugh. I knew we couldn't be anything more and I didn't want to. I grabbed my cheer bag.

"Aight then. Come on," he said, draping his arm over me, but I knocked it off. "You know you gon' be my wife when we get older, right?" he said.

"Not if you're still the same hoe-bag you are today."

"This here, baby girl, is all a phase. I'll be a changed man by the time we get married."

I stood there and closed my eyes. "What you doing?" he asked as he stood there looking at me.

"Trying to picture you as a changed man five years from now and… Nope, you're still going to be a hoe five years from now," I said, opening my eyes.

"That's too soon. Try ten years from now," he insisted. Once again, I closed my eyes and seconds later, I opened them. I shook my head.

"Nope, still a hoe ten years from now."

"Twenty years?" he asked me. I shook my head.

"I'll probably be married to another man by then, dumb-dumb."

"Whatever. It's not gon' take me long to run through all the girls of New Jersey. I'll be done in ten years and will be ready to settle down with my wifey," he said, once again draping his arm over my shoulder. Again, I pushed his arm off of me and then opened my room door.

I checked the hallway before we both walked out and down the hallway.

"Luvleigh Masters. It has a nice ring to—"

"Son of a bitch!" The sound of someone yelling, caused RJ and I to turn around quickly, thinking we were caught, but we didn't see anyone. I recognized the voice as my father's.

"You're in here fucking my wife?" I heard my father say, followed by the sound of crashing glass. RJ and I looked at each other and then ran down to my parents' bedroom.

When we got down there, my father and Uncle Romeo were throwing blows at each other. My mother attempted to get in the middle but was soon pushed out the way so hard that she flew into the dresser. I ran over there to check on her. RJ went over and tried to break the two of them up, but he couldn't do it alone.

I left the room and went to get Tink, who I knew would be by the front of the house, which is where he always was.

Once I told him, he rushed up the stairs and into the bedroom to help RJ. My mom stood there watching, emotionless. I thought maybe she was in shock or something.

They were able to successfully separate the two, but my father continued to try and get after him.

"Get the fuck out my house. Take your fucking kids with you. This partnership is over."

"X, let me explain," Uncle Rome spoke, as blood spewed from his mouth.

"Explain what? How long have you two been fucking?" my dad asked, looking between the two of them. Neither one of them spoke. "Juliet! How fucking long!"

"Baby, please don't do this," my mother begged.

"It's been some time, X, but I swear, we never meant to hurt you."

"You never meant to hurt me, huh?" my father repeated, as he released an inappropriate laugh because this wasn't a funny situation.

We all sat there watching his suspicious behavior.

"I'll leave and give you some time to cool off, X," Uncle Rome said as he and RJ started to leave the room.

They left, leaving my mom, dad, Tink, and I in the room. My dad looked over at my mom and his face twisted up in disgust. It was like everything had slowed down to a turtle crawl, and I stood there, watching in slow motion as my dad grabbed Tink's gun from his holster and walked out the bedroom after Uncle Rome.

Pap! Pap!

My mom and I ran out of the room to see Uncle Rome, laid out on the ground as RJ kneeled over his father, shaking and calling for him to get up.

CHAPTER 2

"So, when was the last time you spoke to mom?" I asked my father as he maneuvered his 2008 Audi R8 through the snow-covered streets of New Jersey. It wasn't often that he got to drive any of his many cars, because he always had people driving him. I don't even know why he wasted his money buying new cars every year. He decided to give his bodyguard, Tink, the night off because his girlfriend had a baby last night, so it was just him and I.

We were coming from his new building for his new music label G.O.A.T. He had just offered this rapper named Tr8z, a multi-million-dollar contract to sign with him. Tr8z was one of my favorite underground rappers, so my dad let me sit in on the signing. I couldn't stop staring at Tr8z because he looked so good. I don't know what it was about him that had me crushing on this man, who was about ten years older than I was. It could have been his music or maybe those light ass, exotic eyes and his tattoo-covered body.

"I haven't," he answered dryly.

"You haven't spoken to mom? Since when? How are y'all supposed to be working things out if y'all aren't even talking?"

"Baby girl, I know you want your mom and I to work things out, but we aren't. She fucked up bad. You're still young, so you won't understand. If she had messed with another man, then we may have been able to work things out. But she messed around with my best friend. My business partner. My brother. Loyalty and trust is everything. You remember that. She lost my trust, and if a marriage doesn't have trust, you can't really call it a marriage."

"So there's no chance that we'll all live under the same roof again?" I asked.

"I doubt it, baby girl."

Since the day my father walked in on my mother and his best friend fucking, which just so happened to be at the same time that I was in my room getting my virginity taken by his best friend's son, he kicked my mother out and like weeks later, my twin brothers went to stay with mother. It was just him and I inside that big ass mansion.

Although he was pissed at my mother right now, he still made sure she was stable financially. The fact that he still cared about her was what gave me hope that my parents would get back together. But it's been a year and we were still living apart.

After my dad shot Romeo, he ended up paralyzed from the waist down. RJ was withdrawn from school and I never heard from, nor seen him after that day.

My father pulled all his money from DYMND records and started his own label, he even took majority of the artist with him. He practically left the Masters broke. I felt bad but fuck it, this was all Romeo's fault. He should have never been fucking my mom.

"Where do you want to stay at tonight? With your mom or with me?" my dad asked as he pulled into the Exxon gas station.

"Daddy, now you know I don't feel comfortable leaving you alone. Of course, I'm going home with you. I have Star and Sun coming over in the morning because I am making you a birthday breakfast."

"You don't worry about me. I'm the daddy. I do all the worrying. If you want to go stay with your mother, it's ok with me."

"And leave you alone on your birthday? I think not."

He shook his head and then smiled.

"Alright. I'll be right back. I need some smokes."

"You don't *need* those things, you *want* those nasty things. There's a difference," I informed him.

"Whatever," he responded, getting out the car. He walked into the mart, and I reached over and turned up the heat and began searching the radio for something to listen to until he came back out. This gave me a little more time to try and convince him to allow my mom to come to his birthday breakfast as well.

I sat back in the seat and closed my eyes as I listened and sung along to Ne-yo's "Miss Independent".

The sound of gunshots caused my eyes to snap open and I looked toward the store. I didn't see my dad anymore, but there were two men wearing hoodies, running from inside of the mart and jumping inside of a blackout Cadi with gold rims.

Once they pulled off, I stepped outside of the car and slowly walked toward the store. I looked inside the window first before going. Once I saw my dad laid out on the floor, I pulled the door open and ran to his side.

"Daddy!" I called, but he didn't answer. "Daddy!" I called once again, and he didn't move. I grabbed his left arm and with all my might, I rolled him over onto his back. Once I noticed his eyes were wide open and the blood that had spilled from the corner of his mouth, I knew he was dead, but that didn't stop me from trying to bring him back to life. I used the CPR routine I learned in school and started to perform it on him.

"No, No, No! Daddy, please don't be dead," I cried. I listened for a breath and checked for a pulse, but there were none. "Daddy, wake up! Wake up for me, please," I begged as I continued to pump his chest to start his heart again. I looked down at my blood-covered hands. "Someone help!" I shouted, but no one came. I continued to yell for help as the tears fell from my eyes, flooding my face, and dropping onto my daddy's body.

"Help me!" I cried, this time shouting louder so that someone would hear me.

This couldn't be happening to me. I couldn't lose my daddy.

JULIET

*D*ressed in some light blue high-waist jeans I got from Fashion Nova, and a white halter top, I slid my fresh pedicured feet into my silver Louboutin's, and then accessorized it with some of my finest diamonds.

My birth certificate said I was fifty-years-old, but the mirror told a different story. I looked twenty-five, maybe thirty at the most. I stood five feet eight, weighing no more than 135 pounds. I had a small waist, nice plump ass, and legs for days. People often compared me to Nicole Murphy, but if you ask me, I looked better. At fifty-years-old, I had men younger than my sons chasing after me.

It'd been ten years since the death of my husband and eleven years since the death of my marriage. I missed Xavier every single day, but I had to pick myself up and uphold the legacy he left behind for our family.

Since his death, I'd taken over the record company, and I'd been doing one hell of a job. He would have certainly been proud of its successes. We brought home three major Grammys for Best Album of the Year, Best Rap Album of the Year, and Best Music Video of the Year. There were no other record companies touching us right now. Not even BRIKZ, which was Romeo's record label.

Since the demise of DYMND, Romeo opened his own record label to compete with X's record label, but being that X was more business savvy, artist gravitated more toward the one who could guarantee them to make the most money. I wasn't X, but I was just as good at making money. I learned from the best.

I sprayed on my Dior perfume and walked out my bedroom that I used to share with Xavier. I moved back in a few weeks after he died. It was hard, but after some time, the days became easier.

I walked down the spiral staircase, and the smell of weed invaded my nose. Shaking my head, I walked downstairs toward the basement.

"What the hell I tell y'all about smoking that shit in the house? I smell this shit from all the way upstairs," I scolded the twins and their friends before reaching for the blunt. Star handed it to me and I took a few pulls before handing it back to him.

"Take this shit outside."

"Sorry, Mrs. Carter," Sun's best friend, Cream said, leaning back into the chair, trying to get a view of my ass. I smiled and gave him a wink. The twins didn't catch that little interaction because they were too preoccupied with that stupid game system. He knew it would have been a problem if they did.

At twenty-six-years-old, my twins were six feet seven, and over two hundred and fifty pounds. You would have thought they asses were Offensive Lineman. They protected our family and our family business. In fact, they were intimidating and very protective of their mother and sister. The only ones to ever try them were the Masters.

It was a never-ending battle between the Carters and the Masters. Since the day X caught Romeo and I having sex in our bathroom, it has been war between our families ever since.

"Your sister will be home in a few hours. I would prefer not to have the house smelling like a fucking Wiz and Snoop party bus."

"Aight, Ma," Sun responded, never taking his eyes off the television screen. I looked over at Cream, whose eyes were still glued on me before I turned and walked back up the stairs. I could still feel him staring at me, so I made sure to put a little twist in my hips.

"Good Afternoon, Margie, what do you have for me today?' I asked my cook, who was in the kitchen. She's been here for more than twelve years. I chose her back when X and I were together. Being a housewife was never a goal of mine, so I hired cooks and a cleaning crew.

"A strawberry spring salad with lemon Dijon vinaigrette and candied walnuts," she replied.

"Nice. How's the vegan cooking lessons coming along? I plan on starting my vegan journey next week."

"As a matter of fact, I'm going to cook small portions of everything I've learned to cook vegan style and have you taste them and let me know if they're to your liking."

"Ok, that sounds great, make enough for four. I'm going to see if I can get Tammy, Ladi, and Luvleigh to take on this new lifestyle with me."

"Ms. Luvleigh is coming home today?" she asked.

"Yes, she's finally bringing her ass home. I was starting to think she thought she was too good to come home to her family."

"For how long?"

"For good. She finished school. Her graduation isn't until next month though."

"That's lovely."

"My daughter is the only one of my kids who chose to actually make something of herself instead of living off her father's hard work," I said as I stuffed some salad into my mouth. "Oh my God, this salad is to die for. Thank you so much, Margie. I'll clean. You can go, and I'll see you later this evening," I told her. She grabbed her purse and stopped to kiss me on the cheek before leaving the house.

I sat there eating my salad and texting my crazy ass sister, Tammy. She said she was on her way over here because she didn't feel like stopping at the store to buy wine, especially when I had a wine cellar over here.

I had to remember to go hide the good shit before she came.

Once I finished eating, I placed my plate inside the sink and went to grab a water from the fridge. When I shut the door, I damn near jumped out my skin.

"Cream, you scared the hell out of me," I said, clutching my chest. "I almost jumped out of my damn skin."

"Oh really? How can I get you to jump out those clothes?" he flirted.

"Oh my God, stop it before one of the boys come up here."

"They won't, they're too busy playing the game. Come here," he said, pulling me inside the pantry and shutting the door. He started to aggressively kiss my neck, which was the way I liked it. I taught him well.

"Oh my God, we can't do this," I said, pushing his chest.

"Why not?" he asked, coming back up and looking at me with those green eyes that made my cougar kitty purr.

"The twins are downstairs," I answered.

"So what. I'll make it quick," he said, turning me around and unbuttoning my jeans. He shimmied them down and then dropped his own pants. I pulled my thong down and then bent my ass over, allowing him access to my pussy.

He poked at my entrance until he was fully inside of me, and he just sat there for a second before pulling out and then pushing himself back in until he caught a rhythm. This little boy knew how to make me climb the walls. He was a year younger than my sons, but he worked this pussy over like a grown ass man. Lucky for me, I was fifty-years-old, and I had yet to start menopause, so my pussy was free to get as wet as it wanted and get beat up whenever I wanted.

The sound of our skin slapping echoed throughout the pantry. I had to reach behind me to tell him to slow it down before we got caught. He pulled me back into his chest as he continued to pump in and out of me while sucking on my neck. His other hand was in the front of me, massaging my pussy.

"Oh shit," he moaned low. "Oh shit," he moaned once more. I bent back over and started throwing my ass back until he grabbed my waist, slowing me down. I knew it was because he was nutting.

Once he was done, we both pulled our pants up. I opened the pantry door and looked out to make sure the coast was clear before we walked out.

"Until next time, Mrs. Carter," he said with a smile before biting his bottom lip and walking out the kitchen.

"Damn," I said, before picking up my water and going upstairs to clean myself up.

∿

I WAS WALKING BACK DOWN the stairs when Tammy came strolling in. She ain't say shit to me, just held up her index finger as she walked into the kitchen. I ain't even have to ask where the hell she was going. I knew she was heading straight for the wine cellar.

I sat down on one of the stools and waited for her to come.

"Yeeahh buddy," I heard her yell. "You got the good shit."

"Damn it," I cursed. Cream had distracted me, so I never got the chance to hide my expensive wine.

She came back into the kitchen and grabbed a wine glass before sitting down across from me. "Tammy, it's not even five yet."

"Girl, it's never too early to indulge in some wine. It's only grapes. Grapes are good for you. Cheers," she said, sliding me the glass she had just filled halfway, and then taking the rest of the bottle to the face.

I laughed at my crazy sister and then took a sip of the wine.

"Whooa, yes, Jesus, take my wheel," she said, bringing the bottle back down from her face and looking at it like it was going to talk back. "Damn, that's some good shit. What's going on sis?" she asked.

"Just waiting on Luvleigh to get in. I'm happy her little ass finally decided to come home."

"I'm sure she's not happy," Tammy muttered before placing the bottle to her lips.

"Why you say that?" I asked her with a slight attitude in my voice.

"Because. She's going from having an independent life without her overbearing ass mother and overprotective brothers, to now coming home and having y'all watching her every move. What if she wants to get her fuck on?"

"What? For one, yo' drunken ass don't know what you're talking about, my baby loves being home with us. She knows we're only protecting her. Two, Luvleigh is still a virgin, thank you so very much."

"Yeah ok. You keep thinking Luvleigh is so innocent. Why do you think she went away to school?"

"To get an education."

"Yup, in dick 101. Niece went away to get her some dick because she knew she was going to stay a virgin sitting around this bitch. Y'all don't let that girl breathe for shit. She went away to school to get away from y'all."

"Luvleigh did not go away to get away from us, and my child is still a virgin, unlike yours."

"Yep, mine ain't no virgin. You know how I know?" she asked, looking at me with her Tami Roman looking ass. "Because my baby tells me everything because she knows she can. That's the kind of relationship we have. My baby girl a bonafide hoe like her momma. Boom," she said, doing a dance like that was something to be proud of. "Just don't tell her father. That dummy will overdose on paint thinner if he knew."

I laughed.

The twins and their friends came walking through the kitchen. "Hey aunty babies," she greeted them as they stopped and gave her hugs and kisses. "My nephews so handsome. I'm surprised y'all ain't got no babies out here yet. These little girls now and days are so dumb. They don't know a come up when they see one. I would have been found a way to trap both y'all ass in my day," she said, with Star's chin in her hand. "I would have been gotten pregnant by both y'all at the same damn time."

"Aunty, how many bottles you had already?" Sun asked her.

"One," she answered, lifting the bottle.

"Before you got here?" Sun added.

"Two... and a half," she admitted, making us laugh. They started walking out to the garage. "Cash rules everything around me, Cream get the money, dollar-dollar bills y'all," she rapped as Cream walked by. "How you doing, Cream?" she flirted, batting her fake eyelashes.

"I'm good, Ms. Tammy. How you?"

"Good," she continued to flirt. "I see you looking at me, kid. I don't think you know what to do with this. This box is more than half ya age baby."

"And? Age ain't nothing but a number. I'll still knock that box out the park," he stated, looking over at me, biting down on his bottom lip before leaving out the kitchen.

"Jesus. They ain't make 'em like him in our day," she said, fanning herself with one of my coasters. "I would hit that. I would hit that hard."

I laughed, turning around to hide my guilty face.

"So what are we doing today?" she asked.

"I wanted to stop at the label first and then go to the mall to get Luv a new wardrobe for when she comes home," I said. Tammy looked at me and then shook her head. "What you shaking your head for?" I questioned her.

"Overbearing. Let's go," she said, grabbing the bottle and walking out the front door to the awaiting car.

LUVLEIGH

"Thank you for picking me up, Tink. I'm happy to see that you're still around," I said from the back seat of the Cadillac Escalade.

"Yeah, so am I, baby girl. How was school? Are you happy to be home?" he asked, looking at me through the rear-view mirror.

"School was great, and I don't know. I kind of enjoyed not being around the madness here."

"I've noticed. Who volunteers to stay in school for an extra two years?" he asked, making me laugh.

"I stayed because I wanted to get my Masters," I answered. I noticed him look at me again and then twist up his lips. "Ok, and I stayed to get away for another two years."

He laughed.

Coming home for good was a bittersweet moment for me. I was happy to be home from school, but I wasn't beat for my mother and brother's shit. I was twenty-four and they still saw me as a little girl. They still thought I was a virgin. That's how oblivious they were to the things that went on in my life. I wasn't a virgin, but I hadn't had sex since the day I lost it. In a way, I felt like my parents splitting up was a consequence for me losing my virginity that day.

My father's death was still unsolved. They said it was a robbery gone wrong, and my father was just caught in the middle. I was the only person there to witness it. Everyone else was dead. They questioned me for like an hour, trying to see if I may have seen one of their faces, but I didn't. The only thing I remembered was the gun I seen the guy running out the store with, and the only reason why I remembered the gun, was because my dad kept one exactly like it locked in his safe. It was a .50 caliber Desert Eagle. He showed me the way around that gun and how to work it. He also promised to get me one in pink, but that never happened because he was killed a few days after.

As I got older, I began to replay the conversations I had with my dad before he died, and it was like he knew he was going to die and was preparing me for those unexpected betrayals in life.

My dad definitely had enemies. I didn't know of any but the Masters, so they were at the top of my suspect list of who may have had something to do with my dad's death.

Since my dad died, my mother took over everything, and she was doing pretty good for the company. She was really representing for G.O.A.T. I was upset that I couldn't make it to the Grammys because I had finals. I did send my congratulations via text message.

"How's everything been here?" I asked.

"Same ol' since you left."

"The Masters still causing problems?"

"More than you know. All I can say is, at least it hasn't gotten violent."

I still couldn't believe how the Carters and the Masters went from being family to enemies so fast. After the years went by, we became strangers to a point that if we saw one another in the streets, we walked passed them like it was nothing. There were a few times when my brothers got into it with the Masters and everyone in the fight ended up battered, bruised, and bloody.

We pulled up to the house and Tink came around to let me out. I walked around and grabbed my pull along Louis Vuitton suitcase, while Tink grabbed the three matching carry-on bags.

"They don't have anything big planned right, Tink?" I asked, trying to prepare for any surprise.

"I don't know. You know we're not allowed in the house anymore. All staff have to chill in the pool house. Only your mom's personal staff are allowed in the main house," he explained.

"What? Since when?"

He shrugged his shoulders.

I shook my head and walked up to the door, twisting the knob and walking inside.

Shockingly, it was quiet and appeared to be empty.

"Hello!" I yelled, walking further inside the house. I expected a crowded house, but I was happy to see that it wasn't.

"Welcome home!" Star came out from behind the wall yelling, scaring the hell out of me. "Oh, was I too early? Fuck, I'm high as shit," Star stated, making me laugh.

"Dumb ass, you were supposed to wait for my cue. Damn, where the hell did I go wrong with you?" my mother said, coming from behind the couch. "Welcome home!" She walked up to me looking as fabulous as she wanted to, and hugged me, which was a little weird being as though Juliet wasn't much of an affectionate person. I guess she was trying to be more motherly.

"Thank you, ma. You look beautiful as always."

"Don't I."

"Aunty Tammy. That wig is giving me so much life. How many bitches you snatched bald for that wig?"

"Just one, niece. The one Spanish bitch from the hardware store that's been flirting with ya uncle. I scalped that bitch so bad, she walking around looking like Fire Marshall Bill."

"Yeah, and you still ain't pay me for bailing yo' ass out," my mother added, making me laugh. Aunt Tammy was the oldest, and although they were sisters, you couldn't really tell. While my mother was light-skinned, almost on the verge of white with gray eyes, my aunt Tammy was a regular, degular brown-skinned chick. They were both beautiful in their own way though. When I was younger, I used to be jealous of Ladi and aunt Tammy's mother-daughter relationship, while Ladi was jealous of the lavish lifestyle that I had. I would have given all that up for a relationship with my mother like the one she had with her's.

"Aunty, I was only kidding. I never expected you to have actually done it."

"I sure did. My Spanish waves popping right?" she asked, swinging her weave back and forth, doing the new Freezer dance. I shook my head.

"Get your mother," I told Ladi.

"Girl, I'm over her ass. You get her," my cousin Ladi retorted with a roll of her eyes. "I miss you, cuz. You know we gotta go out tonight, right, and celebrate," she said, joining her mother in the Freezer dance.

"What? I'm not trying to go out. I don't even have anything to wear and no time to shop."

"Girl, bye. I know you got some cute, rich girl shit in those suitcases."

"There's no need to fear, your mother is here. Told you she was going to need clothes. *Overbearing* my ass. A mother always knows," my mom said, pointing at aunt Tammy and then grabbing my hand, pulling me up the stairs. Ladi and Aunt Tammy followed us.

We got into my room and my momma opened up my closet, and the shit looked like Saks had threw up in this bitch. There were clothes and new shoes, all still with tags. And I'm not talking no cheap shit either. I'm talking Chanel, Fendi, and Gucci. You name it, it was in there. All the shoes had the matching purses. My mother had style out of this world and she knew exactly what I liked.

"Santa," I said, hugging my mother and thanking her for the clothes. I walked back into the closet and hugged all my beautiful new clothes.

"So we going out or what?" Aunt Tammy asked.

"Uh, hells yes we are," I answered, picking up the baby pink Fendi shoes that tied up my calves and had feathers in the front, just above the toes. They were beautiful.

"Good, so let me go get some dick for like an hour and then dump

24

him so I can find me some new-new tonight," Ladi said, followed by some kind of bounce dance.

"Ooeewww," Aunt Tammy cheered as her and Ladi high-fived each other. My mother rolled her eyes at the two of them. "That's my baby," Aunt Tammy gloated. "I taught her well."

"Luv, you still a virgin?" Ladi asked, knowing damn well if I wasn't, I wouldn't say anything in front of my mother. She would probably drop-dead right here in this closet.

"Uh huh," I answered, turning back into the closet so that they couldn't read the lie in my eyes.

"Told you. My child is an angel," my mother said, causing me to roll my eyes where she couldn't see.

"Ok, so where we going tonight?" I asked, changing the subject.

"Pablo is having an album release party, Aunty; you think you can get us in there?" Ladi asked my mother. Pablo was one of the artists at G.O.A.T. His album came out today, so the label was throwing him an album release party.

"I am the Queen, I can get in wherever I want. You two heffas be ready by eleven. I'll go down and tell your brothers. Enjoy your clothes, Luvleigh. I also brought you some new Bath and Body Works, and candles; go take you a nice warm bath. Have a glass of wine and relax. Let's go you two," my mother said, herding my cousin and aunt out the room.

I was finally left alone. I laid back on the bed, limbs spread out. Even with me spread out like a starfish, my king-size bed still swallowed my five feet five, 130-pound frame. I stood up and walked into the closet to find something to wear. I knew I wanted to wear those Fendi shoes, so I pulled out a baby blue latex, one-piece, halter style dress. It matched perfectly with the purse because the Fendi logo on the purse had baby blue in it.

I walked over to the mirror and held the dress up to my body to see how it would look on me and then I pulled my hair up, trying to decide the perfect look that would fit this dress. I decided I was just going to leave it in my signature curly do.

People often said I looked like Bria Murphy, Nicole and Eddie

Murphy's oldest daughter. If you asked me, I would have to agree with them. I could go for her twin sister or something. I may have been a few pounds heavier than she was, but still. I had a very curvaceous thin frame that made every outfit I wore look good. I was built just like my momma, and I hoped I stayed that way, because for my mother to be fifty-years-old, with three grown ass kids, that bitch was smoking fuckin' hot. My daddy was no fool for shooting that club up. She played my daddy though, for real for real.

The clock read 7:02 p.m. I still had time before we went out. I set the room temperature in the bathroom and ran myself a warm bath. Checking out some of the bath foams and salts she had gotten for me, I decided on the coco shea and honey bath products. I wasn't a fan of all that flowery, fruity smelling shit, so this product was best.

I climbed into the bath and sat back, allowing the water to massage my body. I picked up my phone and FaceTimed Hunter. I told her I was coming back home, but I never told her when. I sat the phone up against the body wash bottle so that I wouldn't have to hold it.

"Biiitttccchhh," she answered the phone.

"Biitttccchhh," I mimicked her.

"Biiittccch, why that look like your bathroom?" she asked, placing her face into the phone, trying to get a better look at where I was. All I could see was an eyeball in the frame.

"Because it is."

"You're home? Oh, bitch, I'm on my way,"

"No, wait. What you doing tonight? You wanna come to Pablo's album release party?"

"Fuck yes, I do, hoe. Why would you even ask me that question?"

"Alright, be here at eleven."

"Girl, I'll be there at ten fifteen. What you wearing?"

"Why you always have to know what I'm wearing?" I asked her.

"Because I have to make sure I look better than you. I can't walk in there next to you looking like your maid and shit."

"I can't stand yo' ass. I'm wearing a blue latex one-piece dress and that's all I'm telling you."

"Fine, I'll see you in a few. Bye, hoe," she said, hanging up the phone. I sat there for like another hour. I was starting to doze off, so I got out and wrapped myself in my towel. I didn't even bother getting dressed, I laid on the bed in just a towel and fell asleep. That flight had my ass exhausted.

~

"BEST FRAANNN!!!" I heard Hunter's loud ass voice coming toward my bedroom. I shook my head and continued applying the little makeup my face required. My skin was a smooth peanut butter complexion, and it had a natural glow. I only used a little makeup to cover up the permanent dark mark I had on my face from popping a pimple, creating a scar. I also used some eyebrow gel to darken my weak ass eyebrows. For some reason, my shits would not grow in thick. If there was one thing I didn't leave the house without, that was my damn eyebrows.

"Kaboom," she said, kicking my bedroom door open. "Guess who stepped up in the room," she continued, making me turn toward the door.

"You kick my damn door again and I'm gon' kaboom yo' ass in the nose," I told her. We both stood there looking at each.

"Best Frannn!!" we shouted excitedly in unison as we ran into each other's arms.

"I missed yo' ass. How you go away for six fucking years and only come home twice?"

"I was Facetiming you. You act like you wasn't seeing my face at all."

"Bitch, fuck ya' face. I wanted to see you, hoe"

"I'm here now," I said with a smile, holding my arms out to hug her again. Hunter has been my best friend since I could remember. She was the only one I kept in contact with the entire time I was away at school. My best friend was beautiful. In the looks department, she was up there with me. We were both bomb looking. She resembled Vanessa Simmons in almost every way, except in weight. Hunter was thicker. She had the perfect D size breast, flat stomach, small waist, and the perfect hips, ass, and thigh ratio. She was drop-dead gorgeous. She and her mom were twins.

"Yes, you are," she said, hugging me back. "So what's your plan now that you're home?" she asked.

"As far as what?"

"As far as you getting a job, moving out, finding a man. What's your plan? I know you're not the type to be stuck up under your mother all your life, like your brothers."

"Definitely going to find something to do with my business degree. Not sure what, but I'll figure it out. I always do. If there's one thing I got from my father, it's his business smarts." After my father died and I turned eighteen, I had a private meeting with my dad's ex-lawyer, Henry. I say ex-lawyer because my mother later fired him when he kept giving his input on how my dad's business should have been run, and how his money should have been used. Juliet did not like it, so she fired him just like she fired anyone else who defied her.

But anyway, in this private meeting, Henry informed me of the millions of dollars that was set aside for me alone, once I finished my four years in college. To this day, not even Juliet knew how much money was put away for me. On top of that, I still had my portion of his life insurance money.

While I was in school, Henry helped me invest and buy into stocks, which after some time, doubled the amount of money I had put into it. I was richer than a bitch, and if my dad was alive now, he would have been proud of me.

"It'll probably be some time before I move, and as far as a man, I am not thinking about right now."

"So how long you plan on staying a virgin?" she asked. Like I said before, everyone thought I was still a virgin. There were only two people who knew that I wasn't, and that was the two people who were in the room the night it happened. RJ and me.

"Until I find someone worth having it," I answered.

"Alright Sister Mary, hurry up and finish getting dressed so we can bounce."

I finished applying the makeup and then squeezed into my paint, I mean my dress that was practically fitting like the shit had been painted on. I spun around in the mirror and I looked sexy as fuck. This was definitely going to get people's attention when I walked into that party.

"There you go, always making me feel like a fucking peasant," Hunter mentioned, making me laugh. Hunter didn't come from a lot of money, but she knew if she ever needed anything that I had her no matter what. I helped her get the apartment that she's in now. She hasn't really asked me for anything lately. I guess she was financially stable at the moment.

"I'll take that as a compliment. See, if you hadn't grown that big-ass ass, you could have worn something from my closet," I told her as I tied up my shoes.

"Whatever, I can't help what God blessed me with, shorty. Don't hate."

It was eleven on the dot when we were all piling inside the two trucks and heading out to the city. Hunter, Ladi, and I were in one truck, and my mom and aunt were in another. My brothers drove with their friends.

We pulled up outside of the Sky Room, and you could hear Pablo's music blaring all the way out on the curb. There was a line of people waiting to get inside that was wrapped around the corner.

My brothers stepped out of the car, and all you could hear were bitches screaming their names. My brothers were what you called socialites. People knew them as Juliet Carter's sons, Star and Sun. They got paid to show up at events because they brought the crowds. People knew if the Carter twins were going to be there, then the party was definitely gon' be lit.

A few people called out my mom's name, trying to get her attention, probably to slide her a demo.

Me, on the other hand, I've been out of the limelight, so no one really knew of me, and that's how I wanted to keep it.

We walked inside the party and straight to our VIP section. The party was popping. We had bottles, on top of bottles. I don't know who the fuck they thought was going to be doing all of this drinking. I wasn't much of a drinker because I didn't like that next-day hangover. That shit was for the birds. You would catch me blowing down some trees though. Weed was my thing, not liquor, but I suppose I would have a drink or two tonight.

"This is to you, Luvleigh. Welcome home, baby girl," my mother said, lifting her champagne glass which signaled everyone else to lift theirs.

"Yeah, yo' little nerd ass had to go show the rest of us out with yo' little ass master's degree," Sun added.

"Stop hating and start sipping, nigga," I told him, raising my glass and sipping.

"Now that that's done, how about we go tear up the dance floor," Hunter suggested, grabbing my hand, and I grabbed Ladi's hand, as she pulled us to the dance floor.

My mother, aunt, and my brother, Star joined us on the dance floor where we all danced to Pablo's song, *Summertime Fine*.

Ladi and I danced with each other, while Star and Hunter bumped and grinded next to us. From the way they were going at, they were trying to make me an aunty.

"Them two been fucking for like two years. I don't know why they just don't stop fronting and make it official," Ladi told me. I stood there looking at Hunter and Star and shook my head. That was probably the reason why she hasn't needed money lately. *Alright.*

"I can't believe her ass didn't tell me."

Ladi shrugged her shoulders and then we went back to dancing. With this tight ass dress on, I really couldn't do much. Every time I got in twerking position, I felt my dress rise. It was so dark in here, after a while I just said fuck it and held on to the bottom of my dress and continued to dance, if anyone seen anything, oh fucking well.

"Ah, shit!" I heard Star curse as he pushed through everyone and headed toward the steps that lead up to the VIP area, where we left Sun, Cream, and Merge sitting. I wasn't sure what was going on, but everyone else seemed to know what was going on.

"God damnit, what the hell are they doing here?" my mother asked as she turned around and started to head toward the stairs. Everyone followed her and so did I. I felt like we were walking into a big ass rumble. Either way, I was down for it. It's been a while since I beat a bitch ass.

When we got up to the VIP section, I still couldn't see over my tall ass brothers, but when I got closer, I finally knew what was happening. Them fucking Masters.

"You niggas gotta step," Sun told them as he stood in front of them with his arms crossed.

"We ain't going no fucking where," Leo responded, standing up. Then Aries stood up, followed by their dike cousin, Fatima, and RJ, who might I say, was looking too fucking fine. He resembled Chance the Rapper a little just by his complexion, and the thick pink lips and those low almond-shaped eyes. He had a thick beard that covered the bottom half of his muscular face, that I also found to be super sexy. He wore a black snapback low, almost covering his eyes, with a black short sleeve t-shirt that had the word 'Armani' written in gold. We both stood there, ogling each other. He was looking at me, probably wishing that he was this dress, and I was looking at him, wishing that I was that shirt that hugged his thick chest and those big ass biceps. I did notice the chick who kept trying to cozy up next to him, but he would subtly push her away.

"Yes, the fuck you are. This is a G.O.A.T event, which means you BRIKZ niggas don't belong here," my mother sternly voiced.

"Juliet, why don't you sit yo' fine ass down somewhere and stay the fuck out of men's business," Romeo said from his wheelchair. "Luvleigh, baby girl, I see you're back home, how you been?" Romeo asked.

"Don't you flap them slimy lips toward my daughter."

"The only time these lips were ever slimy, was when you were cumming on them," Romeo said, making my mother, as well as me gasp. "That's how I ended up in this chair, ain't that right?"

"Don't be talking to my fucking mother like that," Star said, punching Romeo in his mouth which started a big ass rumble. All the females were pushed out the way and held back by security until they were able to break the fight up.

The funniest thing was seeing Fatima and Merge going at it. Merge was really getting his ass kicked by a chick. I already knew my brothers were going to clown that nigga for this.

What really got me hype was when the chick that was sitting with RJ, picked up a bottle and smashed that shit over Star's head. I broke away from that security guard so quick, I'm sure all that hoe saw was a baby blue flash of lighting coming toward her. My fist connected with her face so hard, I'm sure I knocked that bitch nose toward the back of her head. Had her ass looking like Olaf the snowman when his carrot nose was pushed out the back of his head.

She started fighting me back, but it all came to an end when she slipped on some liquid that was on the floor. Hunter and Ladi were over there struggling to get out of the grasp of security. I stood over the girl, stomping her with my five-inch Fendi shoes, until I was flung onto the couch by RJ. I was about to get up when more security came and started escorting people out of the club. My mother came to check on me, but I was fine. Besides the little hit in my lip the bitch got on me, I was fine and ready for a rematch.

After the club was cleared out, we sat outside, waiting for our cars to come scoop us up so we could go home.

"You good, sis?" Sun asked.

"Nah, I want that bitches esophagus inside of a jar, sitting on my nightstand," I answered, as I paced back and forth with my hands on my hips. I touched my lip and there was a little blood, but nothing too bad. It was probably going to swell in the morning. I looked up at the passing car and right into the face of RJ. We made eye contact for a second before he looked away, speeding off in his yellow Lamborghini Urus. "Yo Star, I can't believe you hit a man in a wheelchair," I said, laughing. "Yo' ass going to hell."

"Fuck that nigga think he is? Nobody ain't gon' be talking to my mother like that. Now his face gon' be handicap like the rest of that nigga's body."

The cars pulled up and my brothers got inside the car and headed toward the hospital. Star's head was split, so they ended up taking him to the hospital where they had to stitch his shit up from getting hit with that bottle. That bitch was going to pay for hitting my brother.

∽

I woke up the next morning, took a shower and got dressed in my Nike yoga outfit and a pair of Nike sneakers. Hunter said she was going to come with me to a cycling class I found on Groupon.

I walked downstairs and ran straight into my mother. She was nervous and jumpy for some reason.

"You alright, momma?" I asked her.

"Yeah, I'm good," she said, fumbling with her hair. "You look cute, where you going?" she asked.

"To a cycling class with Hunter."

"Nice, have Tink drive you there and tell Star to answer his damn phone. I've been trying to check on him all night."

"I still can't believe them two mess around like that."

"Yeah, well there's a lot that happened since you been gone, Luv. I'll see you later," she said, kissing me on the cheek and then walking up the stairs.

I left out the house and walked straight to the garage. I wasn't about to have Tink drive me anywhere. I'm grown, I can drive my damn self. I removed the tarp from my custom painted purple 2012 Porsche Cayenne.

"Hi, little baby. Momma missed you," I said to my car as I kissed the hood. It's been such a long time since I drove my truck. I loved my car, but as I looked at it, I realized that it was time to upgrade to a later model. I would put that on my list of things to do.

I was pulling out the garage when I noticed Cream sitting inside his car. I guess he was waiting on one of the twins. I beeped the horn and waved at him. He gave me a smile and a head nod. Cream was fine as fuck, in more of a younger Michael Ealy type of way. I would never go there because he was fucking Ladi back when we were teenagers.

I turned on my music and headed toward Hunter's apartment. When I got there, sure enough, Star's car was out front. When I was about the ring the doorbell, the front door came open and Star walked out.

"Good morning, brother," I greeted him.

"What's up, lil' sis?" he asked.

"You tell me, is my best friend, Hunter Willis ready to go get her workout on, or did she already have her workout this morning?"

He laughed. "Nah, she's in the shower now."

"So when was you going to tell me you were fucking my best friend?" I asked him with my arms folded across my chest.

"I mean, if it ever came up, I wouldn't have lied about it. Shit, it wasn't a secret. You weren't around. It just happened," he answered.

"She's sensitive and she loves hard, so be careful with her."

"Who you telling? You know how many times I had to get my fucking car painted because her crazy ass keyed my shit or spray painted my shit. I'm not the one you should be talking to. Her ass does that shit again, I'm knocking her ass the fuck out."

"Stop whatever you're doing to make her go crazy on you."

"Nah, I can't. But she knew about my shit before we started fucking around."

"You niggas are a joke. This is why I'm going to die single and alone."

"Good. That means you're going to stay a virgin," he added, causing me to roll my eyes and step into Hunter's apartment. "Mommy know you're driving?" he asked.

"I'm grown as hell. I don't need to get clearance from you or her. Now ba-bye," I told him, shutting the door in his face while I went to go find Hunter.

I found her in her messy ass bedroom still wrapped in her towel.

"What the hell happened in here?" I asked, picking up the sheets and blanket off the floor.

"You're a virgin so you wouldn't know, but there's a reason why people call it, doing the wild thing. Because shit gets wild. Your brother knows how to put it down, sis," Hunter said, dropping her towel and now standing there ass naked. It didn't bother me though, because we've seen each other naked plenty of times.

"Eww, so I just touched sheets that had you and my brother's body fluids on it. Let me go wash my hands."

"Yep, go on and wash your nieces and nephews down the drain." She laughed as she slid down her sports bra. I did not find anything funny though.

I walked into the bathroom and washed my hands. My fucking lip was all red and shit, which made me mad. I was going to find out who that bitch was.

"Hunt, who was that girl with RJ last night?"

"I think her name is Berniece, and he doesn't go by RJ anymore, girl. That was his teenage name."

"What? Then what the hell he go by then?" I asked, walking into the room. She was completely dressed and now straightening up her mess of a room.

"He goes by Dagger now. Don't ask me why, but RJ is in the past. Dagger fits him. It's sexy just like his ass."

"Dagger?"

"Maybe it's for that thick ass dagger he got between his legs. Shit, he can dagger me with that thing any time."

"Excuse you, bitch. He is the enemy, and must I remind yo' ass that you're fucking my brother. I will snitch on you," I told her.

"You supposed to be my bitch."

"He's my brother. Now, let's go before the class fill up."

"Alright, but we're taking my car because I have an appointment to have my car detailed afterward."

The cycling class was in Glen Rock, so it didn't take us too long to get there. I was used to the intense workout, so I was good, but watching Hunter try and keep up with was the highlight of my life. Once we were done, her legs were wobbly. She would have been good if she hadn't been up fucking all night.

"Bitch, I might kill us trying to drive. I can't feel my legs from this workout," she said before taking off at full speed.

Before going to the car wash, we stopped and picked up some smoothies from GNC.

"Why do you come all the way over here to get your car washed?" I asked.

"Because they're good and they have a wonderful view. You'll love it."

We pulled up to the car wash and waited for our turn. When we were signaled to pull up, and when we did, my mouth dropped open. Now I see what this bitch meant about a view. All the workers were shirtless and wet.

"Oh, my damn," I said, sitting up to get a closer view. Hunter's car windows were tinted so they couldn't see us gawking.

There was a knock on the driver's side window. When I looked to my left, all I saw were gray sweats and a dick print.

"Now, you gon' tell me you wouldn't want this thing to dagger you," she said, rolling her window down. RJ. I mean Dagger's face appeared in the window.

He and I made eye contact and I broke it with an eye roll. "Bitch why would you bring me here. You could have dropped me off at my car."

"Girl, shut up, and just ignore him and enjoy the sausage fest that's before us. My gosh, you're such a virgin," Hunter said as she smiled in Dagger's face, but he was ignoring her and kept looking across at me. He released a chuckle.

"Y'all can get out and go wait in the waiting room," he told us. I grabbed my purse and smoothie before stepping out of the car.

"Where is the waiting room?" I asked. He didn't answer me.

"We're not going in the waiting room. We're going to stand right here and watch."

Dagger got inside her car and drove it up so that they could start working on it.

"Out of all the car wash's, you choose one that Dagger works at?" I asked her, giving her the evil eye.

"He doesn't work here sweetie, he owns this bitch. Now shut up about Dagger and relax."

I rolled my eyes and sat back against the wall, watching all the wet ding-a-lings as they swung back and forth inside their pants while washing the cars. It was like a Gray Sweatpants Matter convention out here. I don't know if that was a part of their uniform or if they were just letting it all hang out because it was hot as fuck today. Either way, I was enjoying it.

"I'm going to go find a bathroom," I said, handing her my purse and setting my smoothie down onto the ground next to her.

After I used the bathroom, I washed my hands and checked my appearance before walking out the door. Or should I say attempting to walk out the door. Dagger was standing there when I stepped out and was pushing me back into the bathroom.

"What are you doing?" I asked Dagger, pushing his hand off me.

"Shut the fuck up," he told me, shutting the door behind him. Once he had me pinned against the wall, he grabbed my face and turned it to the side, gazing at my busted lip.

"Fuck off me," I told him, slapping his hand off my face. "Your bitch did it. I better not see her ass again or I'm fucking her up on sight."

"You ain't gon' do shit to her."

"Aww, aren't you cute taking up for your girl. I promise you, I'm knocking her out."

"That ain't my girl. She's pregnant."

"Then I'm knocking her and that baby out, now excuse me," I said, trying to push past him, but once again, he pushed me up against the wall.

"That was the only reason why I threw you off of her. If she wasn't pregnant with my seed, I would have let you beat her ass."

"Whatever, move."

"Stop acting like you don't like me on you. We both know that you do."

"That was the past, now move the fuck out my way."

"I can't believe you still have your family thinking yo' ass is a virgin. We both know you're not. I still remember the way that pussy felt. I think about that shit often."

"Well, I was a virgin. I'm sure every virgin pussy feels the same."

"I wonder how your family would feel if they knew a Master

deflowered the Carter princess."

"They won't, and if you do, I'll just tell them you raped me. Then I'll go to the cops and tell them the exact same thing. Don't play with me Dagger."

"Word, you would tell the cops I raped you?" he asked with a smile on his face. I nodded my head up and down. "Maybe I should just rape you then," he continued, pressing his body into mine. I felt his hand going down my pants and I tried to stop him, but he was stronger than I was. He grabbed both of my wrists, pinning them above my head and held them there.

"Get off of me, Dagger," I told him as I tried to free my wrists from his grasp.

"You really want me to get off you?" he asked as he successfully got his hands down my pants, and he was now gliding his fingers up and down my slippery slit. He placed his lips against mine, and as much as I wanted to turn away, I couldn't. I kissed him back. The way his soft tongue wrestled with mine, and the feeling of his hands playing with my clit had my pussy salivating. He pulled back. "You don't really want me to get off you," he whispered in my ear. I had to admit, his hands down there stimulating my clit felt incredible, and my body was giving in. I spread my legs just a little, giving him more room to do whatever. I was breaking all the rules right now. If my family knew I was surrendering to the enemy, they would lose their minds. "This pussy is drenched, I don't think you want me to stop."

"I just came from the gym, it's sweating," I told him as I raised my knee and with much force, I kneed him straight in the dick.

"Ah, shit!" he shouted in pain, letting my wrists go and leaning against the wall.

"That's for throwing me, and let your bitch, Berniece, know that I'm looking for her ass," I said before opening the door and walking out of the bathroom.

I made it back out to Hunter.

"What took you so long?" she asked.

"I got lost," I lied as I leaned back against the wall, waiting for them to finish with Hunter's car.

DAGGER

$\mathcal{I}$ sat in my office, icing my dick. Luvleigh's sharp, bony ass kneecaps, fucked my shit up. On top of that, she was looking good as hell, which brought back old feelings I had for her. I suppressed those feelings years ago because I blamed her father for being the reason why my life was fucked up ten years ago.

After X found my father and Juliet getting their fuck on, not only did he shoot my father, but he pulled all his money from the business they shared, leaving the business to struggle financially. My father couldn't do much, being that he was in the hospital recovering, then he had to spend a year in physical therapy. In that time, we lost our home and had to move into a three-bedroom apartment. Once my pops recovered and shit, he was wheelchair bound, but that shit ain't stop him.

He blamed himself for our struggle. He provided my brothers and I with a lifestyle where we were used to getting what we wanted, and we had the best of everything, and that shit was snatched right from under us because he allowed himself to fall victim to Juliet.

My father wasn't used to struggling, so the moment that he could, he got his ass up, figuratively speaking, and got on his grind while in a wheelchair. He managed to rebuild his brand and his reputation. I don't think I've ever seen anyone hustle harder than my pops, and I will forever respect that man until the day I die. Seeing that nigga Star punch my father, had me tight as shit. If Luvleigh's ass hadn't been with them, I would have filled that nigga with lead quick.

I cared for Luvleigh, I always have. Even after her father shot my father, I wanted to go see her. She was all I thought about for about a year straight. While my pops was in the hospital he and I would have one-on-one talks. I even opened up to him about my feelings for Luvleigh. He told me Luvleigh was a great girl, but if she turned out anything like her mother, she would most likely ruin my fucking life, so I chose to stay away from her.

There was a knock on my door before it opened. I looked up and it was 4Dz. She came walking in with her trusty book bag. She never left home without the shit. 4Dz wasn't only my cousin, but she was my best friend. Everyone knew her ass was going to grow up to be a butch. She got more bitches than Aries and Leo. Shit, there were times when she took their bitches.

"Yo, was that bitch, Hunter?" she asked, bopping her Snoop-looking ass into my office and sitting down.

"Yeah, that was her," I answered.

"I'm gon' bag that bitch, her and her big fake ass," she added, making me laugh. "We're the perfect match. She got a fake ass, I got fake dicks. Perfect."

"Yo' ass is wild, cuz. Her ass ain't fake though, Hunter always had a banging ass shape since we were kids. You know, that's that nigga Star, shawty."

"Fuck that nigga. He can't handle that like I can. She needs a real man."

I shook my head at her.

"Yo' ass gon' have us fighting them niggas again over yo' bullshit. Where you coming from?"

"The studio. Aries and Leo got plans for G.O.A.T tonight, you down?"

"I'm always down. You know that," I said, getting up and walking over to the file cabinet with the ice still on my dick.

"Nigga, what the fuck happened to you?"

"Luvleigh's ass kneed me in the dick."

"Damn," she sputtered with laughter. "Kilt yo' shits. You still soft over that bitch?"

"Who me? Nah, I had to put her ass in her place. Talking about she gon' beat the baby out of Berniece."

"It looks like she was the one putting you in your fucking place. Nigga, before you go protecting that bitch, you need to be sure that she's pregnant for one, and two, that that baby is yours."

"I watched her take the pregnancy test, so I know she's pregnant, and as far as it being mine, it ain't shit I can do until the baby comes out. What am I supposed to do? Say fuck her and walk away, and then when the baby comes out looking all Daggered and shit, run back and play good daddy?"

"Yeah, shit. Niggas do it all the time."

"Well, I ain't other niggas, and I'm not a nigga who dips on his responsibilities," I told her, sitting back down at the desk.

"Well, shit, you shouldn't have dipped ya dick in that hoe without a rubber. You can't be like me, nigga. My dicks unsnap, and I can sanitize them before the next use," she said, making me laugh.

"Nigga, shut up. Ain't nobody trying to be like yo' ass."

"Look, speaking of the hoe, I mean yo' baby momma," 4Dz said, nodding her head toward the window at Berniece getting out the car. "I'm out," 4Dz said, getting up and giving me dap before walking out of the door. Once she walked out, Berniece came in. I laughed to myself.

"Hey, baby," she greeted, waddling into the office.

"Sup?" I asked, looking up at her.

"Nothing, my face still hurts."

"You should have minded your business. Nobody told yo' ass to get into it. You should have stayed yo' ass back like all the other women did. Not only did you put yourself in harm's way, you placed that baby as well."

"Don't you mean, *our* baby."

"I mean what the fuck I said, Berniece."

"Well, I was just trying to help. Show you that I'm down for you."

"I appreciate it but stay out of it. I don't need you getting hurt to prove something to me."

"That little bitch wasn't going to hurt me."

"Yes the fuck she was. She was raised around all boys, she knows how to handle herself."

"And so do I, shit. I bet that busted lip put her in her place."

"Yeah, while she's walking around with a busted lip, you're walking around looking like the Elephant Man. Did you put some ice on your face?" I asked her.

"Yeah, I think it went down a little. I only came out to go to the supermarket. I wanted to see what you wanted for dinner."

"You couldn't have called?" I asked her.

"Eww, it's a problem with me coming to your place of business?"

Hell yeah, with ya' face looking like that, I thought to myself. I just shook my head. "It doesn't matter. Get whatever you want. I probably won't make it home until late tonight, anyway."

"Where you going?" she questioned me, causing me to look up at her. She knew I hated that shit, no matter who it was that was asking. I hate when people questioned me. "Whatever, let me go, I'm starting to feel a little nauseous anyway. Can I have some money?" she asked with her hands out. I peered at the palm of her hand.

"What happened to the money I gave you yesterday? I know you ain't spend it all on that cheap ass looking outfit you had on last night."

"That cheap ass looking outfit was Versace. It was nothing cheap about that."

"Whatever," I said, opening my desk and taking out the money pouch. I pulled out three hundred dollars and handed it to her. She looked at it like it was something wrong with the money. "What?" I asked her.

"What is this?"

I gazed at her like her ass done lost her mind. "You know what, you're right," I said, standing up and taking the money back from her, placing it back inside the money pouch. "I'll eat out. Use your own money or find something in the house to eat," I told her, shutting the drawer back.

"What? Did you forget that I am pregnant with your child?"

"And? I'm not even sure that baby is mine. Like I said, there's food in the house, you ain't gon' starve."

She sucked her teeth and stood up. "Whatever, Dagger," she said, then turned and walked out of the office.

I been fucking around with Berniece for like two years now. She got on my damn nerves sometimes, but she satisfied me sexually, and that's all I was using her for. She wasn't wifey material. She was a hoe. That's how I met her, being a hoe. I met shawty at a release party. She had come with the little wimpy ass producer nigga named, Petey. I could tell she wasn't into that nigga, so I snagged her ass up to see what she was about, and shawty volunteered to suck my dick in the bathroom. She sucked my shit so good, my dumb ass brought her ass back to the telly where she fucked the shit out of me, no homo. She had crack pussy. Once I hit it, I kept going back for more. Berniece was fine as hell though. I found it ironic that her name was Berniece, when in fact, she looked a little like the video model Bernice Burgos. She was beautiful, and her body was bad as fuck, but she was bougie as shit and thought her shit didn't stink. She thought everyone that wasn't her, was beneath her, and that shit irritated me. That was one of the reasons why I could never wife her ass. She swore up and down that she was wifey, but she was no such thing. Not even close. I wasn't going to tell her ass that she was only pussy to me until I found another woman to bury myself in. Now that Berniece was pregnant, I had to hold off on cutting her ass off until I found out if that baby was mine or not.

I was messing with this other chick named Maxine that I fucked on occasions, but she wasn't that big of a deal. Unlike Berniece, Maxine wasn't trying to be wifed. At least not by me. She had a husband who she was happily in love with. That nigga just wasn't putting it down how she liked. She loved him, so she didn't want to leave him, so she chose to find herself a side nigga; she found me, who was perfectly ok with being her side bitch. I found it rather funny.

Later that night, I got a text from Leo, telling me to meet him, Aries, and 4Dz on Bunker Hill at eleven. It was already nine when I stepped into the house, so I figured I could just relax on the couch until it was time to go. I wasn't sure what they had planned but I was down for whatever.

Aries and Leo were clowns, pranksters. They often intimidated people by their size, but them niggas were fucking teddy bears. Don't get me wrong, them niggas got down when it was time to handle niggas, but half the time, they were fighting other niggas fights. One time, Aries broke a nigga's back in three places just by placing him in a bear hug. The twins weighed close to three hundred pounds and stood seven feet. People often confused them with the Carter twins, they hated that shit.

I was laying there watching the Cavs and Pacers game while texting Maxine to plan our next fuck session, when I heard footsteps coming down the stairs. I rolled my eyes and sat there, hoping she kept on walking straight out the door and didn't come back for at least a few days.

"Why you are laying down here when I'm upstairs?" she asked, coming around and sitting on the couch with me. I didn't even look her way. That was until she started to tap my leg.

"What Berniece?" I asked, giving her eye contact. I chuckled to myself once I looked at her fucked up face.

"You ain't hear what I just said?"

"Nah, I was watching the game. What you say?" I asked her.

"Why are you not in the bed with me? I'm cold."

"Then turn the air off," I told her. She sucked her teeth. "What? I'm not ready to go bed. I have to run back out in a few, anyway.

"Run out where?" she asked me. I side-eyed her ass.

"What I tell yo' ass about fucking questioning me, Berniece?"

"You still fucking with that bitch Maxine, aren't you?"

"Man, shut the fuck up with that shit. If I was, that ain't none of your business. You ain't my girl. I fuck who I want, when I want. You better be happy I ain't bring no bitch here and fuck her in the bed next to you," I said, getting up and walking into the kitchen. I opened the freezer and grabbed an ice pack before walking back into the living room. "Put this shit on your fucking face." I handed her the ice pack and then walked up the stairs

At twenty-seven-years-old, I owned my own business as well as my own house. When I turned twenty-one, my father gave me the money to buy my car wash. I worked hard and paid him back every cent. My business was so successful that I have plans on opening up two more locations within the next year. As much as I loved my father, I preferred not to live under his name for the rest of my life.

I slipped into my black Nike joggers and a black zip-up Nike hoodie before placing on my black Huaraches. I wasn't sure what the fuck we were getting into, but I knew black would fit the occasion.

I was standing up from putting my shoe on when something hit me in the back of my head. When I looked down on the floor, it was my phone. Before I could even think about what was happening, it happened. I snapped and backhanded the shit out her, knocking her down to the floor.

"Bitch, you lost your fucking mind?" I asked, walking up to her. She sat on the ground, holding on to her mouth that was now dripping blood. I suddenly felt bad for what I had just done. I've never put my hands on a woman, and the fact that she was pregnant made it even worse.

"You're still fucking with that bitch, Maxine," she cried.

"So fucking what, Berniece? I fuck who I want to fuck. You're the one living in my home, not Maxine, so why do you care? I ain't committed to you. Next time you go through my fucking phone again, I will put yo' ass out on the streets," I told her, picking my phone up and strolled out of the room. Berniece must have seen when Maxine texted me back, telling me where and when to meet her.

I read the message and replied 'ok', before grabbing my keys and leaving out of the front door.

When I pulled up to the location where I was to meet my brothers, I was confused as fuck. Once they told me about their plan, I couldn't stop laughing enough to even help these niggas. This shit was gon' be epic.

After breaking and entering G.O.A.T, I pulled up to the address that Maxine sent me and parked under the tree like she asked. I sent her a text, telling her that I was outside. The house she lived in was big as shit. Maxine told me she was a bank manager and I wasn't sure what it was that her husband did, but he had to be someone important because no average person can afford a house like this. When she told me to come to the door, I was confused. She never invited me inside of her home, and now she was inviting me in. We usually got a telly or fucked in the car. That's what I assumed was going to happen tonight.

As I trekked up the driveway, watching my surroundings as I walked, the front door swung open with her standing before me in a silk bathrobe.

"What's up?" I asked with my brows furrowed, trying to see what was going on.

"You," she answered, untying her robe and letting it swing open, revealing her naked body. Maxine was an average looking chick, but baby girl had a body like Ashanti with legs for fucking days, and she was a nympho.

"Where homeboy?" I asked, stepping inside the house. She placed her finger to her lips and then pointed to the ceiling. I looked up and then back at her and then I pointed up asking if he was upstairs. She nodded her head up and down and then shut the door behind me.

"He's suffering from the flu, so I played good fiancée and nursed him with a double dose of nighttime Theraflu. He isn't waking up for a while."

"Damn, you drugged that nigga so you could get some dick?" I asked her.

"Damn right, so why are we still standing here, and your dick isn't inside of me yet."

I pulled her by her bathrobe and into my body as I shoved my tongue down her throat. She started fumbling with the waistband of my pants, pulling them down. She wasted no time in pressing me against the wall and dropping down on her knees, taking my dick down her throat. The feeling of my dick hitting the back of her throat felt good as fuck. I leaned my head back against the wall, enjoying the head I was receiving, never forgetting about the nigga that was only right up the stairs. The house was dark so even if he was to come down the stairs, he wouldn't have seen anything until he got down here and turned the lights on.

I held on to her head as I fucked her throat. Once I was hard enough, I pulled her up by her hair. Digging inside of my pocket, I pulled out a condom, opened it, and tossed the wrapper onto the floor as I slid it down the shaft of my dick. I picked Maxine up, wrapping her legs around my waist as I pinned her back against the wall and started digging her out.

Every now and then I had to cover her mouth to prevent her from screaming out loud. I know she said that he was drugged, but that didn't mean he couldn't wake up. I laid down on the carpeted ground with her on top of me as she bounced up and down on my dick. I reached up, grabbing her titties as I made them bounce as I thrusted my pelvis, pushing my dick deeper inside of her.

"Oh shit!" she shouted as I felt her body tremble.

"Shh," I said, trying to hush her, but it wasn't helping. Her moans grew louder to point that I just said fuck it and continued to fuck her because I felt my nut building up. I rubbed her clit, making her moan as she started to convulse uncontrollably.

"Max," I heard a male call. She stopped moving, but I didn't. I continued to slam my dick inside of her, causing her to moan. I reached up and covered her mouth as I slammed harder and harder until I busted a load inside the condom. I had to admit, it was something about almost getting caught that made this whole thing exciting.

Once I was done, I let her up and I stood up as well. I pulled my pants up with the condom still on.

"Max," he called again. I laughed, pulling her back against my body and kissing her neck.

"One more round?" I asked her. She chuckled before covering my mouth. She then ran up the stairs. I leaned against the door, just in case that nigga came downstairs and I had to get ghost really quick.

I waited for about two minutes before she came walking back down the stairs.

"Let's make this quick," she said, pulling me over to the couch and turning around. I removed the condom I had on and placed another one on as I bent her over the couch and began fucking the pussy up again.

After round two, I kissed her goodnight and went home. That's what the fuck I liked about Maxine. We fucked and kept it moving.

I got home and Berniece was laying in the bed with her back turned toward the door. I went and took a quick shower before getting into bed. I drifted off to sleep but was awakened by a tugging feeling on my dick. I glanced down to see that Berniece had my dick out my shorts as she jerked it, making it grow harder. I removed her hand, but it was replaced by her mouth.

If there was one thing Berniece was good at, it was sucking dick. That's how the fuck I got caught up with her ass.

Grabbing on to the back of her head, I forced myself further down her throat, and she took every inch, regurgitating my dick back up before swallowing again. She was a fucking pro. No one did it like her, which was why it was so hard for me to give this bitch the boot. It would take someone really special to make me trade head like this.

"Damn, girl!" I moaned.

LUVLEIGH

I woke up to my mother standing over my bed and peering down at me. It was a bit creepy when my mother stared because she had some weird auburn, orange-brownish eyes. Almost wolf-like.

"Good morning, baby," she greeted, sitting down on the bed.

"Hey, momma. Why are you standing there looking at me like that?" I asked, sitting up.

"I was just thinking about when you were a little girl and you would ask me to come sleep with you at nights when you were scared."

"That was almost every night when I was seven."

"Yep, and when you turned eight, you were no longer mommy's girl, you became a daddy's girl and only wanted your father sleeping in the bed with you."

"Yeah. I was stingy when it came to my daddy, huh."

"Stingy is not the word. Come on. Get dressed, you're coming to the office with me. I can't leave you alone. You might go out by your-self again."

"Did you forget, I'm twenty-four? Which makes me a grown woman."

"Which still makes you my baby and my child, meaning you do what I tell you to do. Be ready in an hour," she said, walking out the door. I sat there watching as she shut the door behind herself. I rolled my eyes and climbed out the bed, venturing into the bathroom to take a shower. If Juliet thought for one second, she was about to control my life, she had another thought coming.

I showered and got dressed in some high-waist blue jeans and a peach off-the-shoulder crop top that crisscrossed in the front, with a pair of open toe, denim Louboutin's. I wasn't in the mood to do anything to my hair, so I just tossed it into a bun on top of my head.

I made my way downstairs, making sure to make my mother wait at least ten minutes for me. She was standing at the door tight-faced. I chuckled as I placed my Gucci shades on. "Ready when you are," I said, sauntering past her with a smile on my face.

I climbed into the Expedition and sat there, waiting for her to get in. The entire way to the label, I texted Hunter, telling her to come scoop me once she got her ass up. I did not plan on sitting my ass here all day under her watchful eye.

When we got to the label, there was a livestock truck outside the building.

"What the hell is going on here?" my mom asked, jumping out the car before it could come to complete stop. Once it stopped, I jumped out behind her and walked up to the building just as a fucking goat came running out the building.

"What the fuck?" I asked as Sun dashed out the building after the goat. "How the hell did they get in the building?"

"Those fucking Masters. I looked at the security cameras," Sun answered, giving up on the goat chase and jogging over to us.

"Where the fuck they get a bunch of goats from?"

There was animal control, the police, as well as two men with Emai Meat shirts on.

"They were stolen from a slaughterhouse. Do y'all know who's responsible for this?" the police asked as he walked over to us with his pen and notepad, ready to take notes. I looked over at my mother and brother, waiting for them to answer the man. When they didn't, I knew it was because they planned on getting their revenge.

"No, we don't. There was nothing on the surveillance camera," my mother lied.

"Ok, we'll check the cameras at the slaughterhouse and will be in contact with you if we find anything. We'll try and get the animals cleared away as soon as possible," the officer said, closing his notepad and walking back into the building.

"Payback will be a motherfucker," my mother mentioned.

"And I have just the plan," I added as I continued to stand outside, watching them herd away the animals. Once they were done, we walked inside the building and that shit smelled exactly like that. Shit. There was goat shit in the waiting area and throughout the hallways.

My mother called every janitor and cleaning person she could find on such short notice. They charged extra, but she ain't care, she paid them every penny. Shit, if she hadn't paid them, I damn sure would have.

"So what's the plan? Because I'm ready to go knock them niggas out," Star asked.

"We'll need an aerial platform vehicle, some workers, and we'll need someone to go make a hefty purchase from Lowe's. They wanna get petty, so can we," I stated.

"Juliet," my mother answered her office phone.

"Yo, we got goats in the studio recording tracks and shit," Tr8z said. I looked at my mother and brother, and we all chuckled. Those fucking Masters were going to pay for real.

"Tr8z, we had someone play a prank on us this morning. I'll have it cleared out as soon as possible. How about you and the fellas go and enjoy the city, on me. I'll arrange somethings for y'all until we get the studio up to par—"

"Hey Tr8z, it's Luvleigh," I interrupted my mother to speak to my childhood crush.

"Ho-ly shit. How are you beautiful?" he asked.

"I'm pretty good. Back home from school. I heard your latest track. It sucks," I told him honestly.

"Luvleigh!" my mother scolded.

"What? I been listening to his music since I was fourteen. I'm just being honest, Tr8z. I hope you're not offended."

"Not at all. I always appreciate the feedback from my fans. How about you come out to the city with me? It's on your mom. I would like for you to listen to some tracks and give me your honest opinion. I mean, if it's up to your mom."

"Why would it be up to her? I'm grown. I do what I want," I said, peering up at my mother who had an unreadable expression on her face. I knew she was mad, but I didn't care, and I knew she wouldn't have wanted to disappoint her biggest star. "Plus, it's for the label. When my father ran G.O.A.T, he only put out the best. Whoever let that Vertigo track slip by, should be fired."

"Whoa, throwing shade at boss lady?"

"My daughter is just being a little rebellious right now. College life and all. I'll have a car waiting for you outside for you and your guys in ten minutes."

"Nah, it'll just be me and the lovely, Luvleigh."

I smiled as my mother's jaws clenched. "See you in a few, Tr8z," I said, reaching over and hanging up my mother's office phone. "I guess I better go put some makeup on for my date. I mean, business meeting."

"You done lost your fucking mind if you think I'm about to let you walk out that fucking door to go on a date with some nigga ten years older than you," Star said, standing up and blocking my way. Sun stood up as well.

"What are you going to do, tell your biggest star no? You wouldn't want a dissatisfied artist. He might just jump ship," I reminded them. They stood there quietly. "Exactly. Now move," I said, reaching up and mushing them both before walking out of the office door. I sent a text to Hunter, telling her to forget about coming to scoop me and let her know that I would see her later on tonight.

JULIET

I watched as Luvleigh flaunted her little ass out of the office like she had just won something. Little did she know, I was the queen and I ran shit around here. What I say, goes, and it was about time she realized that. She had a lot of say when her father was alive, but he wasn't here anymore, so all that shit was about to stop now.

The bond she and her father had when she was younger, irritated me. Her little ass listened to nothing I said. If I told her no, she would just go ask her father, who would undermine everything. My word meant shit. When Xavier and I first got married, I was his world. He kissed the ground that I walked on, well, whenever he found the time to come home from work. When I had the twins, he dropped rose petals at my feet wherever I walked. I was his moon and stars. Then came Luvleigh, and all the attention I was getting, she had stolen it. Deep down I envied the love he showered her with. There could have been a room full of people, but whenever Luvleigh came into the room, his world would stop, and it would be like no one else existed. Not even the wife who blessed him with her. I was invisible to him, but not to Romeo.

After the second time I had sex with Romeo, I promised myself that I wouldn't do it again. Then I got pregnant with the twins and everything with X and I was amazing, I didn't need to go outside of my marriage. Then Luvleigh came and he stopped giving me the attention that I needed. That's when I started having sex with Romeo again. All the signs of my infidelity were there, he was just so blinded by his love for Luvleigh to realize it. I don't think I need to tell you who named her.

"So you just gon' let her go?" Star asked.

"Yeah, I'll let her do her for now. But sooner or later she's going to fall in line with the rest of y'all."

"And what you mean by that?" Star asked.

"Meaning what I say goes, and by go, I mean go downstairs and have that cleaning crew get down to the studio immediately. If they left, then I guess you two best to get to cleaning," I firmly stated.

"I ain't no fucking maid service."

"You are whatever the hell I say you are, now go. I have shit to do."

They continued to sit there until I gave them a wave of my hand, telling them to get to fucking stepping. The two of them looked at one and another and then stood up before walking out of the room.

I started my morning routine of making calls, paying bills, and getting on artist's asses about the ETAs on these goddamn albums. I was a nice person when it came to business, but there were times when I had to put my motherfucking foot down. I didn't play when it came to my money, which is what my next meeting was about. Putting my fucking Louboutin down on a motherfuckers' neck.

"Mrs. Carter, Mr. Midas is here for your appointment," my assistant Claudette buzzed through. I pressed the button.

"Thank you, Claudette. Send them in. One more thing, do you mind taking a break? You don't have to punch out, I just need some privacy for about twenty minutes?" I asked the sweet older woman.

"No problem, Mrs. Carter. If you need anything, I'll have my cellular on me. See you in twenty."

I pressed the button as my office came open and Claudette was walking Midas into my office with the biggest, cheesiest, ashiest smile on his face like he was all good. It wasn't.

"The Midas Touch is in the building," he said.

"Great, have a seat," I instructed, waving him over to sit in the chair that sat in front of my desk.

"What's going on, Juliet?"

I looked up at him and then back down at the paper on my desk, which was an itemized list of all the money I'd invested into him and where these expenses went.

"Well, Midas, I was informed by your team that you are holding on to the Masters for your album. Do you want to explain to me why that is?"

"No, I don't. I don't have to explain anything to you. I'm the artist. I'm the one that brings the money in. You work for me. I'm sure my team has already explained to you what's up. So why am I here?" he spat, causing my neck to snap back. I was trying to figure out who the fuck he was talking too. He must've really lost his damn mind. It was cool. He was going to learn to fucking day.

"Because, Midas, I would like to hear it from your mouth on why you're dissatisfied with the services my label and I are providing."

"I told you, no album unless I get the rest of my money."

"You do know you signed a contract, right? And in that contract, it states that you received a signing bonus, and then you were going to get an advancement before the release of the album. What's so fucking hard to understand?"

"Hold the fuck up!" he shouted, standing up from his seat. "I don't know who the fuck you think you are talking to."

"I tell you who I'm talking to... You," I said, pausing and then sitting back in my chair. The office doors came open and D-nice and Poo came inside the office. They were like my enforcers. When I say jump, these two jumped and they made sure the world bled on my command.

"Who the fuck is you nigga? Don't you see we're talking business in here?"

The two of them looked at me and I gave them a head nod before they launched at Midas, grabbing his ass up by the shoulders and slamming him on to the floor. Poo held his shoulders down while D-nice pulled down his pants and boxer briefs. I stood up, grabbed something from inside my desk and then slowly walked around to where they were standing.

"What the fuck is going on? Get the fuck off me!" Midas shouted as he tried to wiggle his way out from under their feet.

"Sweetie, you aren't going anywhere. You think you're going to come in my office and speak to me like I don't run shit around this bitch. You must've forgotten, I'm the motherfucking Queen. So, here's how this is going to go," I stated, pressing my stiletto into his dick and pushing the spike of my heel down. "I have here what is called Belladonna, also known as Nightshade. I don't know why it's called that, but it causes dryness in the mouth, difficulty in swallowing, vomiting, excessive stimulation of the heart, hallucinations and if given enough, death. Mmh, pretty cool. This here is venom from a Brazilian Wandering Spider. This causes…" I started reading the label on the valve. "Ouuu, this spider is also known as Phoneutria, which means, murderess. Now, this is dope. I think I'm going to use this one for you. It causes severe burning of the skin, convulsions, hypothermia, blah, blah, and possible death. Great," I said, taking the top off the valve and then sticking the needle into the top.

"No, Juliet, please don't," he begged. I shook my head as I continued to fill the syringe with the venom.

"See, you still don't learn. Even with you're facing death, you're still being disrespectful. Fellas, can you tell this man, my name."

"It's Queen, nigga."

"Yes, it's Queen to you motherfucker."

"I'm sorry, Queen. I'm sorry, Queen!" he started to shout once I placed the needle to his dick.

"Too late. I got the Midas touch now, motherfucker," I said as I injected him with a double dose of the poison and stood back and watched the magic.

After about five minutes of waiting, his body started to shake as white shit fell from his mouth. The spot where I injected the venom started to bubble up and start pussing. D-nice and Poo let him go and he started to convulse, flopping up and down like a fish out of water.

"All you motherfuckers who don't bow to the Queen, will fall. Doesn't matter who you are. Enemy, artist, staff, friend... even family."

Luvleigh

TR8Z and I were sitting inside of Sugar Factory restaurant, talking and catching up. The last time I saw him was the night my dad was killed, and he still looked exactly the same. Fine as fuck. He looked like a thugged-out version of the actor Jesse Williams with his light grayish eyes. His eyes alone could mesmerize you right out yo' drawers, and I wasn't immune to that trance because sitting here, I was ready to toss my panties onto his plate.

"How's that shit you eating?" he asked, making me cover my mouth because I started laughing and I had some food in it.

"Why you have to call my food *shit*, damn?"

"Because who the hell eats all that sugar in the fucking morning? You begging for diabetes or something? You had them melt cotton candy over French Toast that's already covered in all that other syrup and fruity shit."

"It's nothing wrong with my food. It's good. Here, taste it. You can barely taste the sugar," I insisted, forking some of the bread on to my fork and then holding it up to him.

"I don't want that shit," he resisted, turning his head to the left to avoid my food.

"Come on, here, taste it, you can barely taste the sweetness," I continued to insist, getting up from my seat and walking over to him.

"That's because all that sugar got y'all damn taste buds in a diabetic coma. Get out of here with that." He continued to move his head away, trying to avoid my fork. "Girl, go sit yo' little ass down before I bite something else," he said, making me chuckle at his nastiness.

"That's sweeter, so you'll be better off eating this French toast then biting that."

He laughed.

Once he moved over too far to the right, I tipped over just a little, falling onto his lap. He looked up and I removed the food from the fork and quickly shoved it into his mouth. "Gotcha!"

He started to chew the piece of food I shoved into his mouth. Content, I started to stand up, but he pulled me back down and grabbed my chin, bringing my face closer to his and we shared a momentary kiss before I pulled back.

"Are you trying to get dropped from your label?" I asked him.

"If it means I can kiss you again, I don't mind getting dropped. I'm sure I can find another label. Shit, I might get like Gucci and sign to my damn self."

"All of that just to kiss me?"

He nodded his head up and down. "That's what I'm talking about." He pulled my face into his and we kissed again. His lips were soft like rose petals, and his tongue was long and slithery as it invaded my mouth. I loved it though.

The sound of someone clearing their throat caused us to break our kiss. I thought it was the waiter, but it wasn't. It was Dagger.

"Oh shit, what's up Dagger?" Tr8z asked as they slapped hands.

"Shit. Just stopped in to get something to eat. Luvleigh," he said, causing me to roll my eyes.

"Romeo," I responded by calling him by his government name. I stood up and walked back over to my seat. The whole time the bitch I beat up at the club the other day was staring me down. "You have a problem?" I asked her.

"And if I did?" she retorted.

"Bitch, I will stomp you and that baby out."

"Alright, alright, ain't gon' be none of that," Dagger stated as his eyes burned into mine. I guess he ain't like me threatening his baby momma.

"Alright, I'm sensing some tension. Yo, come to Tao tonight. It's a nigga's born day. We bought out the club. Come through," Tr8z suggested.

"Word? Aight, no doubt. I'll be there."

They slapped hands again before Dagger gave me a look and walked away. I picked up my glass and took a sip. I could feel Tr8z staring at me, which made me glance up and catch his stare.

"What?" I asked with a shrug of my shoulders.

"That little gangster side that just came out was sexy as fuck," he responded, making me chuckle. "I take it that the family still beefing?"

"Yes. The goats in the studio. Them," I told him, pointing in the direction that Dagger just walked.

"Word?" he asked, laughing like the shit was funny.

"That's not even funny."

"Kind of is."

"Whatever," I said, throwing a piece of tissue at him.

We sat there talking for a little longer before he waved the waiter over for the check. He paid the bill and we left out.

We headed over to the studio so that I could listen to some of his new album. His music has definitely changed from when I was younger. Back then, his music was about hoes and trappin', but his music now was on the grown and sexy side.

He started rapping along to his music in my direction. He stood up from his chair to stand in front of me before he started to rap softly in my ear.

"Come on, girl put that pussy in my face, I wanna taste that sugar. Don't fight, I won't bite, just let me get my tongue inside it," he rapped as his hands traced my silhouette. He gently bit down on my ear, sending chills down my spine.

The only time I've ever felt like this was the time RJ climbed into the shower with me and started playing with my pussy.

"I see you got a little freak-nasty on this one," I commented, inhaling the scent of his breath because that's just how close to me he was.

"I'm just keeping it real, love. Rapping about what I'm best at."

"And that's what?"

"You want me to show you?" he asked, causing me to giggle nervously, but I didn't say anything.

"The fact that you didn't answer, I'm going to take that as a yes."

He spun my chair around and reached for the button of my jeans, but I stopped him. "You think I'm some easy lay?" I asked him.

"I'm not trying to lay with you, I'm just trying to taste you. You did say it's sweeter than French toast, right? Move your hand," he commanded, grabbing my hand and removing it from blocking access to what he wanted. I had never had a man eat me out. I fantasized about it often but never had it done. I guess it was a first time for everything.

Tr8z unbuttoned my pants and started to lower them. The entire time, he never broke eye contact with me. He removed my shoes, my pants, and then my nude colored thong. He dropped down to his knees in front of me and placed both of my legs over his shoulders, eyeing my waxed kitty like a lion stalking its next kill. He wrapped his hands around my waist and pulled me closer to his face and began licking, slurping, and sucking on my pussy. Whatever he was doing had my body paralyzed. I had never felt anything so pleasurable before in my life. I started spreading my legs, giving him more access. He began licking from my pussy and moved down until I felt his tongue poking at my asshole.

"Oh my God," I cried out as he sucked on my asshole before moving back up to my pussy. I was a virgin to this shit, so once his tongue started fiddling with my clit, my body started to shake.

"Mmhm," he hummed, never taking his mouth off me. I don't know what happened, but the chair suddenly rolled back, and I thought I was going to fall, but instead I was laid gently on the floor. His hands crept under my shirt, where he started to fondle my nipples.

I couldn't believe I was laying here getting ate out by my celebrity crush. I closed my eyes as my body started to shake. For some reason, Dagger's stupid face popped into my head. Maybe because the last time I had an orgasm like this, it was him who was producing it.

"That's right. Let me taste that sugar," he stated before placing his mouth back over my pussy, helping me reach my climax.

I laid on the floor of the studio spent from that orgasm.

"I told you, I'm the best at it," he said as he hovered over me and then bent down and kissed my lips.

"I guess. I mean, I can't grade you, seeing as though that was the first time that's been done to me."

"Stop lying," Tr8z uttered. I shook my head.

"Nope, not lying," I said, sitting up.

"Well, stick with me and there's plenty more where that came from. I'm a master at all things when it comes to pleasing women," he mentioned. I chuckled, followed by a shake of my head as I reached for my thong and started to get dressed.

"Why you shake your head?"

"Because, you just reminded me who you are exactly. A celebrity who has plenty of women at his beck and call."

"And your point?" he asked.

"My point is that, this will never happen again no matter how enjoyable it was."

"That's a lie. I can promise you'll be back for more. There's no other person around that can do what I do. I got skills, Luv," he gloated with a sexy ass smile that made me want to jump on his face again.

"Whatever, can we get back to listening to music, please."

"Be my date to Tao tonight."

"I have plans tonight," I told him.

"All night? Come on. It's my birthday. You really gon' turn your favorite rapper down?" he asked, looking at me and then licking his lips.

"I'll think about it," I stated.

"Nah, I don't want you to think about it. I want you to say 'yes Tr8z, I'll be your date tonight,'" he said in a high-pitched voice, trying to sound like a female. I giggled.

"If I'm done with what I'm doing in time, then yes, I'll come."

"I guess that's good enough."

We sat there talking and listening to the rest of his album. By the time we were finished going over his music, he marked off two songs that I wasn't feeling and said he would go over them with his team to make some revisions. I had been at this studio for at least four hours with him. By the time I left, it was around six in the evening.

The driver brought me back home. When I walked inside the house, my mother and Aunt Tammy were sitting in the living room.

"Well, hello, niece," Aunt Tammy greeted me. My mother didn't even look my way and I didn't care.

"Hello, Aunt Tammy."

"So how was your time with Tr8z? Did you let him hit?" she asked in Aunt Tammy fashion, causing me to chuckle.

"Uh, no. There was no hitting. He did invite me to his birthday party tonight at Tao. Y'all wanna go?" I asked, looking from Tammy to my mom.

"Hell yeah," Tammy answered. I looked over at my mother who was looking at everything except me. I picked up the couch pillow and threw it at her.

"I know you hear me speaking to you, woman. Stop acting like you mad," I said, making her crack a smile.

"I am mad, but I ain't gon' turn down a party full of rich men for no one," she answered.

"Good, let me go call my girls and find something to wear."

"Aye, what about us getting the Masters' back for that goat shit?" my mother asked.

"Mother, if there's one thing I learned from my daddy, is getting shit done. I have it handled. I hired a few guys to do the job for us. So while we're at the party, they'll be doing the work for us. The twins just have to deliver the supplies. The Masters are going to be in for a surprise come tomorrow morning," I stated as I began to stroll up the stairs.

"What exactly is going to happen?"

"You'll see. They should be done by the time we come from Tao tonight."

I got in my room and started searching for something to wear. I decided on my white faux fur lace up two-piece dress, and some silver open toe Giuseppe shoes. This dress was definitely an eye-catcher. It was sleeveless, cropped with a plunging neckline, crisscrossing across my flat belly, and the skirt was sequin, asymmetrical, and stopped above my knees with a faux fur line hem.

I laid my outfit across the chair and then went to take a shower. I wanted to take a nap before the party so that I wouldn't be tired, and I'd be able to enjoy my night.

After showering, I wrapped myself in my towel and was walking out of the bathroom when someone stepped in my path. I screamed just as a hand was placed over my mouth. I looked up and it was Dagger.

Why was this nigga everywhere I was? It was like I couldn't get away from him. Not even being in my own damn room.

"You better not scream when I let your mouth go," he said. I nodded my head, saying that I wouldn't scream. As soon as he let my mouth I started to scream again, but he ended up covering my mouth again before tossing me on the bed. "Didn't I tell yo' ass not to scream?"

I started mumbling words, but he couldn't hear me because his hand was muffling my mouth. He slowly let my mouth go again.

"What the fuck you doing in my room?" I asked.

"Just like old times. You still ain't learn to lock your balcony door?"

"Just because my balcony door is unlocked doesn't give you the right to come through it. You were invited back then, you are not invited here anymore."

"Shut up."

There was a knock on my bedroom door and Dagger jumped up off of me before hiding behind the bedroom door just as it came open.

"You aight, sis? I thought I heard you scream," Star asked, peeking his head in the door. I looked over at Dagger and thought twice about telling my brother he was there.

"Yeah, it was a bee. It flew back out the door though."

"Oh, aight."

He shut the door and Dagger came walking back over to the bed.

"Why the fuck are you here? This is not like old times. You and I are not cool anymore," I said, attempting to get off of the bed, but he knocked me back down.

"You fucked that nigga?" he questioned.

"Why the fuck do you care if I fucked him or not? I ain't the one carrying your baby. You better go and question her ass," I told him again, attempting to get up from the bed, but he knocked me back down again.

"You better not have fucked that nigga, Luvleigh," he said, placing his finger in the middle of my forehead. I hated that shit and he knew that. I knocked his hand away, but he put it right back there.

"As a matter of fact, I did. I fucked him hard. That was the best dick I've ever had."

He looked at me through squinted eyes.

"Lying ass. You better not fuck him. That nigga got dick herpes."

I sucked my teeth and pushed him off me. "You are such a hater. I used a condom," I said, successfully standing up from the bed. I walked over to my dresser and removed a pair of shorts and a tank top before slipping them on. I tried to play it off like I wasn't worried about it, but deep down, I was. I thank God, I didn't let that nigga hit it. *Eww, I kissed him and let him eat my pussy.* "What you walking around worrying about another nigga's dick for anyway?"

"Girl, ain't nobody worried about that nigga. I just came here to let yo' ass know about that nigga. I know you didn't fuck him, Luvleigh, and you need to keep it that way," he told me as he started to walk back toward the balcony door.

"You ain't my damn daddy."

"Why would I want to be? He's dead and I'm alive," he said, making me gasp in shock. I couldn't believe he said that. Actually, I can because he was an inconsiderate bastard just like the rest of the Masters. I picked up the picture that was next to my bed and threw it at him, but he quickly shut the balcony doors, and the picture frame crashed into it, breaking. I laid back on the bed, gazing up at the ceiling. I picked my phone up and started to research about Herpes and how it spreads. There was no way I could have contracted Herpes, seeing as though Dagger said he had dick herpes and not mouth herpes. I still wasn't about to take any chances. I was calling my Gyno first thing tomorrow morning. Fuck that.

DAGGER

*O*nce I made it back to my car safely, I drove back home. I knew I was risking my fucking life by popping up at the Carter's house, but I needed to warn Luvleigh about ol' boy. I knew it sounded like I was hating on the nigga, I was, but I wasn't making that shit up though. I cared about Luvleigh. Always have and always will. Seeing her kissing that nigga, fucked me up for some reason, and I didn't know why. I hated her family, which meant I should hate her ass too, but I didn't. Seeing her the first night she came home from school, triggered feelings I had felt for her back when we younger.

I drove home rocking to that Cardi B and Chance the Rapper song. I don't know why, Cardi B's ass annoyed the fuck out of me, but it was a dope track.

Pulling into my driveway, I glanced up at the bedroom light which was still on, and I rolled my eyes. I was hoping her ass would not be here, or at least sleep, shit. I got out of the car and reluctantly walked toward the house.

When I got in the bedroom, she had outfits and shit laid out on the bed.

"Hey babe," she greeted me with the biggest smile on her face. As beautiful as it was, I was about to wipe that smile off her face.

"What's up?" I asked, walking further into the room. "Where you going?" I asked her.

"To Tao with you," she cheerfully stated.

"Who said?" I asked, sitting down on the bed.

"Excuse me?"

"Who said you were going? Tr8z didn't invite you. He invited me. You're not going."

"What you mean, I'm not invited? I'm never invited anywhere, and you still take me. What's different this time?"

"Yo' ass ain't going and that's the end of that. So I suggest you start putting all this shit back inside ya bags."

"Wait, hol' up. Why you suddenly acting funny with me? What changed?"

"What changed is that I don't want yo' ass hanging all over me tonight. As a matter of fact, I don't even want you in my house. No offense, but you gotta go home. I'm about tired of you being here. Yo' ass don't never go home. I'm not paying rent on that motherfucking apartment for you to be up in my ass all the time. Nah. Go home, Berniece! I'll get at you tomorrow," I told her, kicking off my shoes as I began to undress.

"It's that bitch, Maxine, isn't it?" she asked with her hands on her hips.

"What? No, it's not Maxine, damn. Why you always bringing Maxine up?"

"If it's not her, then who? Who is it Romeo?" she shouted.

"Who the fuck are you yelling at? You know what, I'm not doing this shit. Leave or I'm dragging yo' ass out my fucking house."

She stood there tapping her foot with her arms folded across her chest. I turned around ignoring her, walking into the bathroom to take a shower. I shut the door behind me and proceeded to take a shower. I just prayed that she wasn't still here when I got out of the shower.

I knew the way I spoke to her was fucked up, but sometimes you just have to rip the fucking band-aid off. I wasn't trying to play house with her ass. I just wanted to take care of my kid, if it was even my kid. That was the only reason why I continued to pay her rent and give her money.

I got out of the shower and wrapped a towel around my waist. I was happy to see that she wasn't standing there anymore and all her clothes that were on the bed were gone. After getting dressed in only a pair of basketball shorts, I went downstairs to chill a little before I went to Tao. As I got downstairs, the sound of running water coming from the kitchen caught my attention. I traveled into the kitchen and the sink was overflowing with water.

"What the fuck!" I shouted as I ran over to the sink and turned the water off. "This stupid bitch," I said as I stuck my hand into the soapy water to drain it. My hand hit something hard. I started moving the suds out of the way and when I saw what was submerged in the water, my skin began to seethe. "No, the fuck she didn't," I said as I lifted my Xbox from under the water. Once again, I reached down into the water to drain the sink and I felt something else. I picked it up and it was my fucking phone. Dumb bitch thought she was doing something. My shit was waterproof. "I'm gon' kill that hoe."

I walked back to the living room to sit down on the couch and dry my phone off. I opened up the message thread and sent Berniece a text message, telling her that I was going to fuck her ass up when I saw her.

My phone vibrated, it was her texting me back.

B: Whatever, you own a car detailer, I'm sure you can fix it. Maybe next time you'll think twice before speaking to me like I'm some random ass bitch.

Car detail? I thought to myself before looking out the window at my Lamborghini. It looked fine from here. I walked outside to make sure my car was good. After going around to the back of the car, I saw that the bitch had keyed up my fucking car. For fucking what though? Because I told her to leave. This bitch done lost her fucking mind.

"I'm killing that bitch."

I walked back inside of the house and called 4Dz to tell her what the fuck Berniece did. I knew her ass was going to have a lot to say because she was the one who told me not to bring that bitch into my home. She warned me, and I didn't listen.

～

TAO WAS POPPING. There were bitches and bottles everywhere like it was the theme of the party. I'm glad I didn't have Berniece hanging all over me because I spotted at least two bitches I was trying to get into tonight. I expected to see Luvleigh's ass here, but I guess after I told her about homeboy, she decided not to accompany him to the club. Her little ass tried to make me jealous by saying she fucked Tr8z, but I could tell her ass was lying. She wasn't even like that, but then again, I didn't know what she was like anymore. I knew the Luvleigh from ten years ago, when we were teenagers feeling up on each other every chance we got.

"Damn, the bitches in here tonight are baddies for real," Leo said as he watched the dancefloor from behind his LV shades.

"Word, I'm about to go see what's up with shorty with the blonde hair," I told them, never taking my eyes off shorty as she swayed her ass back and forth to Rich the Kid's New Freezer. From the face to the small waist, and the thick ass, she resembled that chick Alexis Skyy.

"Look at this shit," 4Dz said, before putting the bottle to her face. I looked in the direction she was looking, and Luvleigh, Juliet, Tammy, Ladi, and Hunter came walking over. I don't know why 4Dz was surprised, I told her Luvleigh was going to be here. I guess it was surprising that they were here without their bodyguards. All that shit didn't matter though because that dress Luvleigh was wearing commanded all attention. Every nigga that was sitting on this couch right now, was eyeing her ass in that dress.

Even the nigga, Tr8z, who just seconds ago, had like three bitches in his face, was now salivating at the sight of Luvleigh.

"What a fucking way to make an appearance," Tr8z commented as he stood up and walked over to her. He went to kiss her on the lips, but she turned her head, playing it off like she was looking at something else. I knew it was because of what I told her about him having herpes. They were just slobbing each other down earlier at the restaurant.

"Thanks. I told you, I had other things to do," she spoke, looking my way and catching my eyes as they danced across her body. I'm sure her brothers ain't see what the hell she had on when she left the house. I would have never let her ass come out the house dressed like that.

"You have an eye problem, Dagger?" she asked, making me look up at her.

I shook my head at her because I wasn't about to get into it with her ass. I knew I would get verbally jumped by her and her entire entourage. I picked up my bottle and walked over to the chick on the dance floor that I had been eyeing all night. I walked up behind her, wrapping one arm around her waist and pulled her body into mine. She turned and looked up at me ready to go off. Once she saw me, I guess she was satisfied with what she was seeing because she smiled and wrapped her arms around my neck.

We danced as her girls stood around watching us like we were the king and queen at a fucking ball. After one dance, that shit was starting to get on my nerves. "Y'all wanna come chill with me and my nigga?" I asked the girl who I now knew as Nyia'lee, and her friends.

"Yeah, we can do that. I'm sure Shamara would love to sit down. Her dogs are probably screaming right now," Nyia'lee joked, making everyone laugh except for the girl, Shamara.

"Fuck you, bitch, because you are so right. These are not my dancing shoes," Shamara said, and I waved the three girls to follow me.

"What's your name, shorty?" I asked the other girl.

"Karen," she responded. I nodded my head.

When we got back to the VIP section, I introduced the girls to my brothers and cousin. 4Dz already zoomed in on Karen.

Luvleigh and her entourage were over there in the faces of Tr8z and his niggas. Luvleigh was talking to Tr8z, and the way Tr8z was touching on her legs had me in my damn feelings just a little.

"I'm sorry but I'm not into girls," Karen said, knocking down 4Dz's advances.

"Who the fuck said I was a girl? I'm a nigga," 4Dz replied to her.

"Well, I like dick and unless them shits grow magically, I'm pretty sure you don't have one."

"Who the fuck said I ain't got a dick? They don't call me 4Dz for no reason, baby."

"And what reason is that?" Karen inquired, making me shake my head because I already knew what was about to happen.

4Dz removed her backpack from her back and unzipped it. She pulled out her trusted silver case and opened it. Every time she opened that case, I felt like there should have been a bright yellow light that appeared, as if she was revealing a golden treasure.

"They call me 4Dz because I have four dicks. One in every flesh tone, what's your dick preference? White, waffle colored, brown skin or Wakanda?" 4Dz asked, causing everyone to laugh, including Tr8z and Luvleigh, as she picked up the black strap-on dick that she called Wakanda.

"Oh my God," Karen squealed with her hands covering her mouth. I'm sure that was not what she was expecting.

"Don't look shocked, baby. I know how to use these shits too. Me and Wakanda will have yo' ass climbing the fucking wall like Spiderman."

"Yo, put them shits away," I said, slapping her ass in the back of the head.

"What? Shit. Bitches be trying to play me out," 4Dz stated, putting her dicks in the case before slipping it back inside her trusty backpack.

My fucking cousin was wild as shit and had no fucking filter what-so-fucking-ever. She was my cousin but was more like a brother. 4Dz has been living with us since she was fourteen. Her mother, who I had never met, was allowing her boyfriend to molest 4Dz since the age of eight. When my pops found out about the shit, he paid my aunt Ilene a hundred grand to allow him to take custody of 4Dz. The fucked up part about it was, that it only took her all of twenty-two seconds to agree to give her daughter up.

I guess you can say, being raised around a bunch of boys made her into the butch she was today. She and I were the same age and were interested in the same things. That was getting money and bitches. My brothers weren't trying to do shit with themselves but live off of my pop's money. Not me. Suds and Dubs was my pride and fucking joy.

4Dz owned a strip club called Double Dz out in Newark, New Jersey. The shit was popular with the locals, but it wasn't a big deal. I've been trying to encourage her to expand her shit and start getting some celebrities to come out to the shit to help bring in some more money. Shit, my pops had musical artists falling out his ass. Shit, if she wanted, I could get the bitch Brit Brat from Love & Hip Hop to make an appearance at the bar. She's an ex-stripper turned rapper, and willing to do anything to get a shot at stardom. 4Dz ain't give a shit though. As long as the ass and titties were perfect, that's all that mattered.

I sat there chatting with the chick Nyia'lee. While she spoke, my eyes danced over her smooth, peanut butter complexion, and my mind was already envisioning the sight of her bare ass bent over in front of me.

"Why are you looking at me like that? You're making me nervous," she said, once she noticed I wasn't paying attention to nothing she was saying, whatsoever.

"You look like you taste like a Reese's Cup," I answered.

"I do, you want a taste?" she asked, sticking out her arm, then playfully pulling it back when I made a biting gesture.

"Bite that damn arm off, girl. I'm about to run to the bathroom. Wait right here for me, aight?"

"Ok. Make sure you wash your hands."

I chuckled, jumping up from the couch and walking to the bathroom. I stood at the urinal pissing when the bathroom door came open. I paid no attention to who it was until two people stood on both sides of me, simultaneously. It was Sun and the nigga Cream that he always be with. They must've just got here because I ain't see their asses the entire night.

They pulled their dicks out and started to use the bathroom. I kept on doing what I was doing, not the least bit worried about the two of them. Neither one of them were about that life. Now, if it was Star, then that would have been a different story. Star would have popped off immediately, like that fuck nigga did to my pops. I was still salty about that shit. Just for that, I should go back out there and smack the shit out their mother with my dick on some Jamie Foxx shit.

As I'm standing there taking my piss and shit, I felt the nigga, Sun, looking over at me.

"What the fuck you looking at?" I asked him.

"At pussy, that's what the fuck you are," he answered.

I ain't say shit. I tucked my dick back into my pants and backed up.

"Then pop the fuck off then, bitch. Oh, I forgot, you ain't shit when your brother ain't around."

"Shut the fuck up, nigga. Tonight ain't the night, but best believe next time, yo' ass gon' be on the ground leaking."

"Nigga, the only thing that's gon' be leaking is my nut down your mother's throat," I responded with a devilish smile. Unexpectedly, the nigga Cream jumped at me before Sun did, and it was *his* mother. Sun held him back from almost getting his ass beat.

I confidently turned around and walked to the sink to wash my hands before I left out of the bathroom.

When I got back to the section where everyone was at, the sight before me had me heated as fuck. The steam coming from my ears could have been seen from miles away. Not only was I mad that Berniece was here and in Niya'lee's face, but she had the nerve to bring her ass here after I told her not to come; and the fact that she thought shit was all good after what she did to my fucking car.

I stomped over to her.

"What the fuck you doing here?" I asked, pushing her away from Nyia'lee. 4Dz was already standing between the two of them as Nyia'lee stood there, unbothered.

"Excuse me. What you mean what am I doing here? What you

doing here all up in this bitch's face, when I'm sitting home pregnant with your child," Berniece said, making a big ass fucking scene. I rubbed my hands down my face because I was really about to embarrass this bitch if she didn't take her ass home.

"Bitch, do I look like I'm playing with yo' ass right now? After the stunt you pulled with keying my fucking car, you lucky if I don't lay yo' ass the fuck out in this club. Take yo' ass the fuck home, and I don't mean my house, I mean yo' fucking apartment. And since you wanna come here causing a scene, pack ya' shit and go the fuck back to sleeping on your mother's couch. Until I find out that baby is mine, I'm done providing for your ass," I told her as I went and sat back down on the couch.

"Are you fucking serious right now, Dagger?"

"Do I look like I'm fucking joking with ya' ass? As a matter of fact."

I searched the area until I found one of the bouncers and then waved him over. "Yo, get her out of here. Escort her ass out to the curb," I told the bouncer. He gave me a head nod before grabbing Berniece by the arm and walked her away from the VIP section.

Looking around, all eyes were on me. Including, fucking Luvleigh.

"Fuck you niggas looking at? Go back to whatever the fuck y'all were doing."

"Excuse you! Nigga, your bitch was just escorted out the club, so better check ya' fucking self," Luvleigh commented while doing that neck roll, head snap shit that these bitches be doing, looking like a bunch of fucking llamas.

"Luvleigh, don't fucking start with yo' shit. Go back to being up in that nigga's face."

"What you jealous that she's up in my face, instead of mixed up in your shit?" Tr8z asked, causing me to turn around. "I see the way you been eye-fucking shorty from over there."

"Nigga, ain't nobody eye-fucking her. I don't need to eye-fuck Luvleigh. If I wanted to fuck, I could. I already hit it once and if I wanted to hit that shit again, I would."

I heard a few people gasp for air. I looked around and noticed Juliet, Tammy, Hunter, and Ladi's mouths all open. I guess the secret

73

was out. Their little precious princess wasn't as pure as they thought.

"The fuck you just say?" Star asked, standing up from the couch. Sun stood behind him like always, waiting for go time. When Star stood up, Leo, Aries, and 4Dz stood up as well because they already knew what time it was. This shit never got fucking old. This rival shit was routine for us now.

"You heard me. What? You thought yo' little sister was innocent? Nah, nigga. I been popped that fucking cherry, nigga."

Before I could say another word, Star came charging at me, wrapping his arms around my lower half and lifting me up into the air. I started throwing elbows into his back, causing him to drop me back down to my feet and from there, we started going at it like Rock 'em Sock 'em Robots.

We ended up getting put out the fucking club like always. I don't know when this feud shit was going to come to a head, but I knew the moment it did, somebody or bodies were going to end up dead. Personally, I didn't feel like it should have had to come to that. We were family before all this shit. My family was salty because of the way X almost left us without a father and how he left us, the boys that he called his nephews, to struggle. He did us wrong, and now that he wasn't here, his family was feeling our rage.

The Carters, on the other hand, I had no idea why they exuded so much hate toward us. It was all Juliet though. Word around the industry is that she blamed us for X being murdered. Claiming that she knew we had something to do with it, and we were going to pay for the death of her husband.

My pops told us to stay clear from the Carters and we tried, but it seemed like wherever we went, they were right there, and shit always got dicey.

LUVLEIGH

*A*fter we all ended up getting put out of Tao, the ride home was quiet. My mother sat there staring out the window the entire time. I knew she was mad at hearing that I wasn't a virgin. I couldn't believe Dagger had outed me in the way that he did. Not only was my mother mad, I knew my brothers were going to be pissed too.

"Tink, can you stop by BRIKZ?" I called up to the front of the car.

"Sure thing, baby girl," he agreed, and then went back to focusing on the road.

"No, Tink. Please take us straight home," my mother interjected, speaking for the first time.

"Yes, Ms. Juliet."

"You don't want to check on the job that's been done at BRIKZ?" I asked her. She ignored me and kept on looking out of the window. I figured I would leave her be and not try and speak to her anymore.

Tink dropped my cousin and aunt off at their home, and then took my mom, Hunter, and I back to our house. Hunter's car was at my house, but she would probably end up staying with Star.

When the car pulled up to the house, we all hopped out. My mother walked straight into the house and upstairs into her room before slamming the door shut. As expected, Hunter went straight into Star's room and I traveled into my room, removing the dress I had on. I didn't change into my pajamas. Instead, I put on some tights, a regular t-shirt, some Jordans, and grabbed my wallet and keys before jumping into my car and pulling off. Thanks to Ladi, I knew exactly where I was going.

It was already three in the morning. Kinnelon wasn't too far from Ramsey, so it only took me about twenty minutes to get there. I knew it was risky coming here, but I was pissed off.

I climbed out of the car and walked up to Dagger's house door. Once I was standing in front of it, I turned my back to the door and started kicking as hard as I could, and I didn't stop until the door swung open and I almost fell inside the house.

Dagger was standing there with a scowl on his face, but I didn't give a fuck.

Wham!

Now he had my hand print along with that scowl on his face.

"How could you?" I asked him. His scowl turned into shock from how hard I had just smacked him. He grabbed my arm and pulled me into his house so hard, letting me go and I fell down to the floor.

He slammed the door shut and walked up to me, grabbing me up by my t-shirt before flinging my ass onto the couch.

"Put your fucking hands on me again, Luvleigh, I will break that shit off," he warned me, strolling away. He came back into the living room with an icepack on his forehead and sat down on the couch across from me. He was shirtless and in a different situation, I would have been marveling at the sight of his chiseled abdomen, but I was pissed off right now.

"Why you do that? Why would you tell my mother and brothers about us having sex like that?" I asked him.

"You acting like I lied on yo' ass or some shit. What the fuck you so shook for, Luvleigh? You a grown ass fucking woman. They need to realize that shit and stop trying to dictate your fucking life."

"You don't get to determine that. Who the fuck are you, Dagger? You had no right. That was my fucking business to tell," I yelled, picking up a water bottle that was sitting on the coffee table and throwing it at him. It hit him in the chest. He looked up at me and threw down the ice pack before marching over to the couch that I was sitting on. I knew I had just fucked up by the look in his eyes. It was a scary one.

He snatched me up by the throat, lifting me up in the air. This was not what I was expecting when I made the rash decision to bring my ass here.

Dagger stood me to my feet. "Didn't I tell you to keep your fucking hands off of me?" he asked, placing his finger in the middle of my forehead. He knew I hated that shit. I slapped his hand away as he backed me up against the wall.

I don't know where it came from, I guess I got turned on by being roughed-up, but I wrapped my hand around the back of his neck and pulled him closer to me and began to kiss him. After a few seconds, he pulled back, unlatching from the kiss and just stared at me.

"What are you doing?" he asked.

"Kissing you," I answered.

"Well don't," he responded, slamming me against the wall but not hard at all. He let me go and walked back over to the couch to sit down. He laid his head back onto the couch and just peered up at the ceiling. I couldn't help myself. I walked over to the couch and straddled his lap. When he didn't push me off him, I got comfortable and leaned forward, and kissed his lips. When he didn't pull back, I continued to kiss him until he started to partake in the kiss. He wrapped his arms around my waist and tugged me into him.

His cologne invaded my nostrils, turning me on even more.

He stood up from the couch with my legs wrapped around his waist and then laid me back down on the couch as he got comfortable between my legs. He reached down and removed my sneakers from my feet, never breaking our lip-lock.

We continued to kiss each other like we were two lovers who haven't seen each other in months. He broke the kiss as his soft, wet tongue grazed against my neck, gently sucking my skin into his mouth and then releasing it. He wasn't sucking hard enough to produce a hickey, but it was firm enough to cause a reaction down under.

His hands traveled under my shirt, and he gently began to twist my nipples between his fingers. I had no bra on, so when he ripped my tank top, my little perky C cup titties bounced out. Dagger's mouth made a smooth transition from my neck to my titties. His tongue flicked across my nipple, driving me in-fucking-sane. I moved his head over from my right titty to my left, and he did the same thing.

I pulled his shirt over his head, tossing it behind the couch and then reached between our two bodies to unbutton his pants. I hadn't had sex in years and hadn't wanted it, but here I was ready to get it in. I don't know what it was about Dagger that just made me want to give him my pussy, yet again.

I used my feet to lower his pants down further and then his boxer briefs. He sat up on his knees and then placed both of my legs together in front of him. With that Dagger smoothness, he slid my tights and panties right from off my body.

I went to open my legs, but he held them closed, pushing them into my chest, as he planted his face into my coochie. At the first few lickings, my body shook vigorously. Right then and there, I knew my ass done fucked up. The more I tried to pull away, the tighter his lock around my thighs got. *Tr8z's head game had nothing on Dagger's,* was what I thought before he went from teasing my clit, to daggering his tongue in and out my hole. *Damn, I got head twice in twenty-four hours by two different niggas. I was that bitch.*

"Stop fucking running. You grown, right? Act like it and take this licking," Dagger told me in an authoritative tone that made me stop pushing, and just lay there and take it. With the grip he had on my thighs, he was able to control my body, moving it up and then down on to his tongue.

"Oh my God!" I cried out loud.

"Oh ya God what?" he asked, coming up from between my legs. His lips glistened from my juices. He went to kiss me, and I pulled back a little because he had my pussy secretions on his lips, but he still managed to press his face into mine. After I tasted my sweet nectar on his lips, I kissed him back with just as much passion. Shit, my juices made the kiss even better.

I was so caught up in the kiss, that it never crossed my mind to brace myself when I felt him tapping at my entrance before sliding into my tight hole.

"Fuck!" I shouted out from the feeling of him invading my pussy for the second time in years. Ten years to be exact.

"Damn, you still feel the same from the first time."

"How can you remember that? That was so long ago."

"That was a day I can never forget," he said as he slowly stroked in and out of me, opening me up enough for his dick to get some good strokes. Once he had his opening, he took off, punishing and pleasing my pussy until we ended up on the carpeted floor. "This shit is tight ass fuck, Luv," he moaned in my ear and I smiled.

Dagger lifted his body off mine and sat back on his knees. He gripped my legs and turned me around with ease. I suddenly became nervous. I didn't know what to do in this position. All I knew how to do was lay on my back.

"Why you shaking?" he asked.

"I've never been in this position before," I revealed, but I'm pretty sure he already knew that.

"Just relax. I'll try not to hurt you, Luv. I promise."

That was all it took to ease my spirits. He pulled me up on to all fours and pushed down on my back to create an arch. He angled his dick at my opening and slowly pushed himself in before he started pounding at my ass. The pain soon turned into pleasure as the sounds of the wetness that my pussy had created, and the sound of skin smacking, echoed throughout the room. Before I knew it, I was partaking in the sex by throwing my ass back to match his thrusts. There was a point where he had to grab a hold of my waist to slow me down. I was so in my zone, that it was him trying to keep up with me.

"Yeah, that's what I'm talking about Luvleigh. Throw that ass back," he told me as he swiftly stood onto his feet, never missing a beat or a thrust. He got a few thrusts in before he fell back down to his knees. He tugged my body closer to his so that we were now chest to back, and then he bit down onto my shoulder as he continued to pump into me.

"Shit, I'm about to cum, Luv," he mentioned.

"Ok, just make sure you pull-out," I told him. He didn't respond, he just placed his face into the crook of my neck as he moaned in my ear.

"Fuuckk!" he cursed, as his thrusts picked up and his teeth sank into my shoulder. Dagger reached around and started to manipulate my pussy by rubbing my clit repeatedly until I felt myself reaching my climax. "Shit!" he shouted, as he pushed me up and then pulled out of me, letting his nut squirt out onto the carpet.

He stood there jerking at his dick until every drop of the sperm was out.

We sat there naked for a while, with our backs against the couch. Neither one of us said anything. It was getting a little awkward, so I stood up and started to get dressed. After a few seconds, he stood up as well and pulled his pants up. I placed my Jordans back on and walked myself to the door. I didn't realize he was behind me until he reached in front of me to open the front door.

"Don't bring your ass to my house again," he stated. My neck, in a natural reaction, jerked back.

"Don't flatter yourself, nigga, I didn't plan on coming back to your shitty ass house anyway," I threw back at him right before the door slammed in my face. "Bitch ass," I uttered before turning and walking to my car.

The sun had started to rise. I knew my mother was going to be all in my ass with the questions. I truly wasn't in the mood for her shit.

DAGGER

*a*fter Luvleigh left, I gathered my shit and walked upstairs. When I got into my room, I was damn near scared half to fucking death by Berniece sitting on the bed with her arms folded across her chest.

"Oh shit! What the fuck are you doing here? How long have you been here?" I questioned.

"Oh, right before you took her down to the floor," she answered, looking at me through squinted eyes like she was mad at me for something.

"How did you get in here?"

"Through the window. I've been sitting here for almost two hours."

"So ain't nobody tell you to bring your ass over here. Now you can get the fuck out too."

"What? I am pregnant with your child, you can't kick me out," she said. I guess it was up to me to prove her the fuck wrong.

I sat my shit down and walked over to her ass, scooping her up like a baby. She didn't start fighting back until I got to the front door. She started flailing her arms and legs, smacking me in the face, and she even bit down on my chest

"Ahh!" I screamed as I dropped her ass straight on her ass to check my chest. This bitch done broke my skin. I was pissed. I pulled her to her feet, forcefully dragging her outside of the house and shut the front door. Berniece started to kick and scream at the front door, and I had no plans on opening the shit either.

I went upstairs to take myself a shower. I undressed and looked down at my dick that was still wet from Luvleigh's pussy juices. *Damn.* After all these years, I was still weak for that girl, but there was no way her and I could be together, especially not with her fucking mother.

Yeah, our families didn't get along, but that was all because of Juliet. She wasn't trying to squash shit, whatsoever. She manipulated her kids into thinking we were the enemy and that we were the ones being difficult when in fact it was the complete opposite.

I stood in the shower a little longer, allowing the water to run through my mini fade. I rubbed my chest where Bernice had bit me, attempting to clean it out before I was to dress it with a bandage. I really couldn't believe her ass sat up here, listening to me fuck Luvleigh. The fact that she didn't interrupt it was weird, which told me she had something up her sleeve. I turned the shower off and wrapped the towel around my waist.

I walked out into the bedroom, which was dark, although I don't remember shutting the lights off. I paid no mind to it, I just flipped the switch back on. When I did, there was a figure sitting up in the bed with the cover over their head. I knew it was no one but Berniece, but my question was, how the fuck did she get in? Again.

"What the fuck, Berniece?" I asked, pulling the cover off of her head. She sat there smiling like shit was funny, but I found nothing funny. I wanted her the fuck out of my house. "How did you get in?"

"I'll never tell," she said, mimicking Brittany Murphy's character from the movie *Along Came A Spider*. I quickly walked up to the bed and smacked her upside the head.

"Do it look like I'm joking with yo' ass?"

"Oh my God, damn, Dagger. I climbed up the waterspout and through the window."

"What? Who the fuck are you? The Itsy-Bitsy Spider? Get the fuck out my house," I told her.

"Nah, I'm not going anywhere. You can't just put me out like that. You acting like I mean nothing to you, Dagger. I am the mother of your unborn child, and I want to be here with you."

"Well, I don't want you here, so you need to go."

"No!"

I shook my head and walked over to my closet. I slid into some clothes. When she saw me come out the closet fully dressed, her mouth dropped open.

"Where are you going?" she asked, sitting up in the bed.

"Away from you. If you want to stay here, then you stay in this bitch by yo' damn self. I'm out," I told her as I walked out the room and down the stairs. I heard her coming down behind me. I quickly grabbed my keys and my wallet before jogging out the door and to my car.

I pressed to start the car and was pulling off by the time she had gotten to the door. I was going to stay at my father's house for a while. She ain't know where he lived, so I wouldn't have to worry about her ass climbing fucking waterspouts over there.

LADI

I was on my way home from last night's booty call. I was definitely going to hit that shit again. That nigga had me ready to snatch my motherfucking edges out my damn scalp the way he laid the dick down. Not to mention, this nigga was famous and had money falling out his ass.

It was going on seven in the morning and I knew my mother would be up by now and had breakfast waiting. She was a fucking early-bird. Don't matter how much she drank or smoked the night before, or whether she stayed out all night cheating on my daddy, she was always up, and breakfast was on the table. I loved my momma dearly.

I pulled up to my house and was surprised by a cop car in the driveway, blocking me from going in.

"What the hell?" I asked out loud to no one in particular. I climbed out the car and walked through my front yard that was now decorated with my mom's wigs. I was walking closer to the door before I was popped on the top of my head by one of my mom's Christian Louboutin stilettos, causing me to look up.

"Daddy, what you doing?" I asked as a bunch of clothes rained down on me. I removed my mom's button up Versace shirt from my head. "You could have killed me with that shoe," I told him.

"I'm sorry, baby girl, but your momma gotta get the hell out my house."

"Wait, what?" I asked with a hint of laughter in my voice, because last time I checked, this was my mom's house.

"You heard me, that skank gots to go."

I laughed as I walked inside of the house. I guess he finally found out my mother was a hoe. Sorry to say, but she was, and she knew that shit.

"Ain't nobody going no fucking where, lil' nigga," my mother yelled from the bottom of the stairs while an officer guarded her from running up them. My father was only doing this because my mother was being held back. He knew that if that cop wasn't here, my mother would have tossed his ass out of the house faster than Uncle Phil tossed Jazz out from the *Fresh Prince of Bel-air*.

My father only weighed like 120 pounds, while my mother weighed a good 160, but she was super curvy. My mother was a bad bitch for real for real. I guess it was in our family genes because my aunt Juliet was drop-dead gorgeous, and Luvleigh was beautiful as well. People often confused the four of us as sisters, but we were a mother-daughter combo.

My father's little Katt Williams-looking-ass came running down the stairs and stepped into my mother's face. "I bet the fuck you are," he stated. My mother's face screwed up right before she reached over the officer and bitch-slapped my daddy. She hit him so hard, I felt that shit.

"Momma!"

"So fucking what. I'm the man and the woman of this house. What I say goes."

The officer grabbed my mother. "Ma'am, I'm going to have to place you under arrest for assault," the officer said, grasping my mom's wrists and hooking a handcuff on one and then the other.

"That's right, lock her ass up and throw away the key. I hope you become somebody's bitch up in there."

I looked over at my daddy and for the first time, I noticed the colorful marks on his nose as well as something that looked like silver-like nail polish.

"Daddy, you been sniffing the markers agai—"

"Noooo," he answered, cutting me off. He stood there like a four-year-old who just got caught doing something he ain't have no business doing.

"Yes the fuck he was. I caught his ass up there huffing fucking spray paint. That's why his nose looks like he's been eating the Tin Man's ass."

I started laughing. *Oh my God, my parents are fucking wild.*

"Bitch," he cursed, as he ran up to my mom and snatched the lace front she had on her head off, and then ran to the door to toss it out with the rest of her wigs. This shit was fucking hilarious. My dad really looked like Katt Williams when he was on video getting beat up by a teenager. His hair was all over his head, he was sweating, and out of breath.

"Motherfucker," my mom cursed, taking off after him and then bum-rushing him to the ground. I really felt bad for this officer. He was going to need fucking back up.

With her arms behind her back, and her stocking cap struggling to hang on, she laid on top of my father's body. She reached her face down and bit his chest.

"Ma'am, stop it."

"Momma, he's going to take you to jail. Cut it out," I told her. She stopped her no-hand assault and attempted to pull herself up from the floor. With the help of the officer, she was successfully on her feet. "And daddy, you stop provoking her."

"Ain't nobody provoking that hoe. She just a drunken hoe, who can't keep her pussy in her panties."

"Oh my God, why me?" I asked with my hands over my face. I just been fucked bald and all I wanted to do was come home, shower and go to sleep, not referee my parents.

"I wouldn't have had to fuck other men if your dick worked. You been sniffing all these fucking fumes, you turned your dick into a fucking crackhead too."

"Fuck you!"

"That you couldn't do, Crack Head Dick."

"OMG! Officer do you have to take her to jail? Can you just take her to my aunt's house? I'll make sure to keep them two separated."

"Your mother just assaulted him in front of me. If your father isn't going to press charges, then I can release her."

"He's not."

"Yes, the fuck I am," my father responded, and I looked over at him to see that his facial expression was dead ass serious.

"He's not, officer. He's just in his feelings and he's a little high off the fumes. I'll personally escort my mother to my aunt's house and tell security not to allow her out the house."

"Ok, if there's another incident then I will not hesitate to take both of them in for disorderly conduct."

"There won't be another, I promise."

The officer gave me a head nod and then walked out with my mom in handcuffs. I unlocked the car for her to get in and then I turned to my father.

"You really should be ashamed of yourself, daddy. You really was going to send your wife to jail?" I asked, side-eyeing him.

"I damn sure was. Lil' tramp. Ain't no dick inside the pen. I was hoping her ass got turned out by a big butch named Bob," he said, walking upstairs.

"Daddy, you better not be up there sniffing that spray paint again, and make sure you clean that yard up before the neighbors banish us from the neighborhood!" I yelled up the stairs after him. He didn't respond. He just kept on walking.

I shook my head and walked out the door. Before reaching my car, I stopped and snatched up my mom's wig that she had on before my daddy yanked it off of her head.

When I got inside the car, my momma was sitting in there breathing heavily like she was ready to jump out the car and run back into the house, but the officer was still standing by his car, waiting for us to pull off.

"You good, momma?" I asked her, handing her the wig.

"Oh, thank you, baby. You always look out for your momma," she answered, taking the wig from me and then placing it back on her head any ol' way. I laughed before pulling off.

DAGGER

"*P*ops, what's up?" I asked, walking into the living room. I really hadn't gotten much sleep. I arrived at my father's house ten minutes to seven and only got about forty minutes of sleep. I still had a room here and probably always would. Surprisingly, my father was very nurturing and caring, and he was overprotective of his kids. He was like Father Goose.

When I moved out, he hated that shit. I don't think I've ever seen my father cry before until I moved out. He said it was because he couldn't protect me like he would be able to if I was under his roof.

Everyone looked at my father as this mean, ruthless nigga, but he was the opposite. That was all a guard to make niggas aware and not to fuck with him. If my pops needed to be, he could get ruthless. He did some fucked up shit back in the day and fucking his partner's wife wasn't even the worst of it. My father and X were mayhem when they joined together as one. That DYMND record label they put together years back, was built from conquest, war, famine, and death. That record label should have been named apocalypse instead of DYMND. Juliet was their downfall. I don't know how my father fell in love with that woman.

"Wondering why you're here instead of at your home," he

responded, looking down at some paperwork. My father resembled the actor nigga, Terry Crews. With his bald ass wrinkled head, dark skin, and his tight lips, he could easily go for a twin brother of Terry Crews.

"Fucking Bernice's ass won't leave me the fuck alone. I told her I wasn't beat for her shit and wasn't trying to be with her. If the baby was mine, then cool, I'll be there, but if she thinks that's going to make us a couple it's not."

"I understand, but you can't hide out here. You have to handle yo' shit. Put ya' foot down. You can't tell her you don't want to deal with her, and then turn around and lay the dick on her. You gotta make a clean cut from her, and that you can't do because she's pregnant with yo' kid—"

"Allegedly," I blurted, cutting him off. "I'm still not sure if that's my baby."

"Well, until you find out, you will continue to be there. I didn't raise you to skip out on your responsibilities."

"I'm not trying to skip out, I don't want to be with her, but I do want to be there for my kid. I pay for her apartment, I put food in that bitch mouth. What the fuck else do I need to do?"

"That's what you young'ns don't understand. It's not always about material things, it's about being supportive and understanding of what they are going through."

"Pops! Does that even sound like Berniece? That bitch is only about the material shit. I don't like her vibe."

"Does this have anything to do with Luvleigh being back in town? I told you to stay away from that girl. I don't have anything against Luv, but her mother is a conniving bitch with a grudge for the Masters."

"Nah, it has nothing to do with Luvleigh. I ain't thinking about that girl," I lied, when in fact, she was all I could think about since she left. Sex with her just felt different. It was like, I wasn't just fucking her, I was making love to Luvleigh. I didn't want that, but I couldn't help that she brought out uncharted feelings I had inside.

"Yeah ok. You coming into the office this morning?"

"Yeah, let me just go jump in the sho—"

"Ohh shit! My dicks!" we heard 4Dz shout from upstairs. My father's house was 6.9 thousand square feet, which mean this shit was big as fuck, and 4Dz's bedroom was the furthest to the back, so you can imagine how loud her ass had to scream for us to clearly hear her.

My father and I both looked at each other confused. We heard her bare feet patting down the hallway and then stomping down the stairs. She came up to us with her book bag held open.

"Where are my dicks, man? Somebody got me for my dicks," she cried like Martin cried when he told Gina to step. The bitch was coming out of her, and this shit was so funny, I couldn't help but laugh. "Call the cops, I been robbed. Man, nooo, somebody stole my dicks." She continued to cry as she fell out on the couch. She was really crying real tears.

"What you mean somebody stole your dicks? Who would steal your dicks?" I asked.

"Nigga, if I knew, do you think I would be standing here? Why the fuck y'all ain't calling the cops? I've been robbed for my dicks," she said, making dramatic hand gestures which made this scene extra fucking hilarious. My pops couldn't do anything but sit there and look at her with his hand covering his mouth, trying not to laugh. We all knew how passionate she was about her little dicks, so as funny as this was, we knew she was truly hurt.

"4Dz, we can't call the cops. What the fuck we gon' say? Keep a lookout for four missing dicks?"

"I don't give a fuck what you say to them niggas. They gotta find my dicks, man."

"When was the last time you seen them?" I asked.

"Last night when I pulled them out for the bitches and then you told me to put them back, I did. The fight broke out and I put my bag down, after the fight, my bag was still there, but it never dawned on me to check and make sure my dicks were there. I mean, who would steal my dicks, man. They were innocent, man."

I draped my arm around her shoulders and pulled her into my side as she covered her face, trying not to cry. I tried really hard to suppress the urge to burst out laughing.

"It's all good, cuz, we'll find them," I told her as I rubbed her back.

"They're probably all scared and shit," she added, and that was it. That suppressed laughter that had built up inside of me came out, and I fell out laughing. She really was convinced that these fucking silicone dicks had feelings and shit.

"You think this is a big fucking joke, right. I got ya fucking ha-ha's and he-he's, nigga."

"You right, it's not funny, niece, we'll find them. How about you go get dressed and come into the office with us. You know, help get ya' mind off it," my pops suggested.

"Nah, man, I need to mourn my loss," she said, as she dragged herself back upstairs. I looked over at my pops and we both quietly laughed. I left him alone to go take a shower.

ROMEO

After Romeo Jr. finally got his ass out of the shower, which took for fucking ever, we headed to the studio. He drove behind my 2018 Mercedes Benz Metris Luxury van that I had customized to my liking. Yeah, I could have gotten a car, but I wasn't going to have any man lifting me out of my chair and placing me in the car like some fucking incompetent gimp. Although I was in fact handicap, I never wanted to be treated like one. So when it came to me getting where I needed to go, I preferred they just rolled my chair into my van and kept it moving.

Although the doctors told me that I would never walk again, it never stopped me from trying. I went to physical therapy twice a week, but it was only proving that the doctor was right. I would never walk again.

I looked in the rearview mirror at my son's Lamborghini as he drove directly behind us. Romeo Jr. was my fucking pride and joy. He was the only one out of my sons that had his own mind. The only one who wanted to make a name for himself instead of continuing to live off my name and legacy. When I first heard that he had a baby on the way, I was overjoyed until I remembered who was carrying his seed.

Berniece's ass was scandalous, but I could tell she really loved my son, he just loathed her, with a passion.

My cell phone rang, and it was my artist, Tron. I picked up immediately. He was my top selling-artist, so I wanted to make sure all of his needs were being met.

"T-Raww, what's good, son?" I greeted him.

"Ro-me Rome, we can't get out," he spoke. My head jerked.

"What you mean you can't get out? Get out of where? Don't tell me y'all niggas in jail again."

"Nah, nah, nothing like that. The building doors won't open."

"What? I'm on my way in anyway. I'll be there in five minutes," I told him, hanging up the phone. "Rudy!"

"Sir," he answered.

"We have a problem at the studio, I need you to push it, man."

"Sure thing. Hold on, sir," he said, pressing on the gas before I could grab on to anything. My wheelchair rolled to the back of the van, hitting the back doors.

"Shit!" I cursed. "I think you gave me whiplash, nigga. Shit!" I rotated my neck back and forth.

"Sorry, sir, I told you to hold on," he said with a hint of laughter in his voice.

"Yo' ass did that shit on purpose. Think you slick, nigga," I responded as we both joined in a laugh.

Rudy has been with me for about eight years. He was actually X's bodyguard, but when X died, Juliet fired him which was the dumbest shit she could have done. This nigga Rudy and Tink was with X and I from the start of it all. They were loyal as hell, and I would trust these niggas with my life. Once Juliet fired him, he came straight to me for work, along with everyone else her ass fired. I couldn't hire everyone at the time, but I did hire most of them.

Within two minutes the van was coming to a sudden halt, which caused my chair to roll to the front. "Goddamnit! Yo' ass about to get fucking fired."

"Sir, you have a problem," he said, as he sat hunched over the steering wheel, looking up at the building. I glanced over at the building and instantly became pissed off.

"Get me the fuck out the car!" I ordered as Rudy jumped out of the van and came around to let me out. Romeo Jr. was getting out his car at the same time and he started walking to the building. We both stood th—well he stood, I sat, there looking at the bricked-over building.

Someone had bricked BRIKZ. The entire first level of the building where the front and back exits were, had a layer of bricks going around it, preventing anyone from getting out and anyone from going in. This was some bullshit. I looked over at Romeo Jr., pissed the fuck off.

"This is all you and your brother's fault for putting them god damn goats in G.O.A.T," I told him, with my finger pointed at him. He laughed like something was fucking funny. "You find something funny? Because I damn sure don't. What if there was a fire? We would have some burned up fucking rap stars in that bitch."

"It wasn't my idea, you need to go yell at Leo and Aries' ass."

"You participated, you're the oldest, and you the only one here right now so I'm going to get on yo' ass. Fix this shit, Romeo. Now!"

"How the hell am I supposed to fix this?"

"Nigga, I don't care if you have to throw ya big ass head into the fucking building to knock them shits down. Fix it. I'm going to get my dick sucked," I told him as I turned my chair around and started rolling back to the van.

"Pops!" Romeo Jr. called.

"What?" I answered, never turning toward him because I already knew he had some stupid shit to say.

"You know your dick can't feel shit, so why the fuck you keep paying bitches to suck that limp noodle?"

"Mind yo' motherfucking business. It's called wishful thinking, asshole. Let me know when this shit is handled."

I heard him laugh, but I ignored him and rolled back to the van.

LUVLEIGH

"uck!" I cursed as I lifted my head off of the pillow. I looked at the time and it was two in the afternoon. I can't believe I slept this long. I got in around five and stripped down and climbed straight into the bed. I didn't even wash my ass.

I sat up and for the second time, my damn creepy ass mother was sitting there. "Why is it that you're always sitting here when I wake up? It's like you can sense when I'm about to wake up," I said to her as I stood up out the bed in just my tank top and thong and started fixing my bed.

"I can sense something alright. I can smell him all over you. That's where you been? You been out fucking? Who Romeo Jr.? You told me you were a virgin, you lied to me."

"Mom, please. Nobody lied to you. You just wanted to believe what the hell you wanted to believe. It was ten years ago. I only had sex that one time."

"You should have not been having sex at all, Luvleigh! Ever!" she yelled. I side-eyed her at the same time that natural neck jerk happened.

"Last time I checked, I was over the age of eighteen, meaning I'm a grown ass woman. If I want to fuck, I'm going to fuck, and no disrespect mother, but there's nothing you can do about that."

I finished making my bed and sauntered into the bathroom.

"You do what you want, little girl, but you will not be fucking a Masters. They are responsible for the death of your father, and I will be damned if my daughter is fucking the enemy."

"Momma, there is no proof that they had something to do with my daddy's death. You're the only one who's placing blame on the Masters."

"Because I fucking know!" she shouted, pointing at me. "Now get in the shower and wash that stench off of you. You stay away from Romeo Jr. He's a walking venereal disease just like his fucking father."

I waved her off and went to get in the shower. I ain't have the time to deal with her ass right about now. She done brainwashed everyone into thinking the Masters murdered my father, but I wasn't convinced. I blamed them for my father's death in a whole different way. I didn't personally think they were the ones who held the gun, but I do think that if Romeo Sr. hadn't been fucking my mother, then my parents wouldn't have split, DYMND wouldn't have been torn apart, and my father wouldn't have been out that night coming from G.O.A.T. That was why I resented them so much because of their father.

After I got out the shower, I got dressed in a pair of jeans and a regular shirt before deciding to find something to eat. I heard my aunt Tammy's voice, as well as Ladi's, and I was glad because I wasn't beat for my mother scowling at me the whole time.

"Hey, Aunty. Hey, cuz," I greeted them as I went and sat in Ladi's lap.

"Bitch, get off me. Yo' ass out here keeping secrets and shit," Ladi said, pushing me off her lap. I slapped her on the knee and then got back up and sat on the arm of the chair. For the first time, I noticed my aunt's appearance. Her wig was lopsided. The bang was over her left ear and she sat there like that shit wasn't fucking with her. It had to be, because it was fucking with me and it wasn't even on my head.

"Auntie what happened to you? I'd never seen you look like this."

"Girl, I almost killed your uncle Byron's ass," she answered, picking up the almost empty bottle of wine and sipped directly from the bottle.

"What? Why?"

"Girl, them two were going at it. He had my momma's wigs scattered all over the front yard, like snow," Ladi answered, causing my mouth to drop open.

"Not ya wigs, auntie."

"Girl, yes. Then had the nerve to snatch the one I had on my head off and throw it out the front door. That nigga was only acting tough because that cop was there—"

"Wait, there was a cop?"

"Hell yeah," my aunt answered with a roll of her eyes.

"Why did this happen?"

The both of them sat there quietly. I looked between Ladi and my aunt Tammy, waiting on one of them to answer.

"Because your aunt is a word that rhymes with joe," Ladi answered, making us laugh.

"Watch your mouth. I'm still your mother."

"And you're still a—" Ladi whispered "hoe" and we both started laughing.

"Whatever. Nobody told his ass to be nosy. Sniffing my drawers and shit, fucking bum," my aunt vented. "I don't know how he smelled anything with all that spray paint jam packed up his nose."

"You married him," my mother added, picking up her glass of water and sipping.

"Because he had a big dick," my aunt retorted, causing me to stand up.

"This is where I excuse myself and go find myself something to eat," I said with my finger up.

"I'll come with you," Ladi volunteered.

"Why? From what I hear you was out getting dicked down last night, too!" my aunt shouted, and I ignored her and kept on walking into the kitchen.

Margie was in there standing over the stove. I was happy because that meant I didn't have to cook for myself. I couldn't cook for shit because I never learned. I grew up privileged, with cooks and chuffers at my beck and call. My father taught me how to drive when I was twelve though.

"Hey, Margie. What you cooking?" I asked, walking over to the stove where she stood.

"Some vegan sweet potato casserole with pecan crumble," she told.

"That looks good. Can I taste?" I asked her.

"Sure."

She scooped some of it into a spoon and held it to my mouth, like she would do when I was younger. "Oh my God, that's so good. Can you put me some of that in bowl? I am starving."

"I wanna taste," Ladi said. After she tasted that deliciousness, she too wanted some.

"You know your mom was trying to get all of you to go vegan. Looks like she's going to get her way," Margie spoke, making me roll my eyes.

"She always finds a way to get her way."

I went and sat at the island with Ladi, while we waited for our food. She kept looking at me all weird and shit like she wanted to ask me something.

"Why the fuck are you sitting there looking all weird and shit. Out with it."

"So were you out getting some dick last night?" she finally asked. I looked over at Margie, who wasn't paying us no attention.

"I was."

"From who? Dagger? It was Dagger, wasn't it?" she eagerly asked.

"No, it was not."

"Yes, it was. Who else would you be out here fucking?"

"Tr8z," I lied.

"Now, I know that's a fucking lie."

"It's not a lie. It was Tr8z," I continued to lie.

"When did you become such a liar? College has changed your ass for the worse. What happened to my innocent cousin?"

"I still am innocent. I told you it was Tr8z. You're just choosing not to believe me. Anyway, who did you end up going home with?"

"It's a secret. I can't tell you."

"That's so fucked up, for real. I told you who I was with last night."

"No, you lied. I can tell you're lying, but it's cool because I already know it was Dagger."

"What makes you so sure?"

She pulled out her phone and started scrolling. After a few seconds, she turned her phone toward me. It was someone's Facebook page. I looked at the name and it was the Berniece chick. Her status read, *when you walk in your home and find your man fucking another bitch, but it's all good. I'm the one that's carrying his child and spending the cash. #unbothered #babyMasters #wegoodoverhere #Imwifey #yourejustconvenientpussy #TheprincessofGOATisahomewrecker #smackinbitchesonsightall2018.*

My mouth dropped open and I instantly became heated. I started to read the comments where someone asked why she didn't smack me when she walked in on us? But she didn't answer. I wasn't for this social media shit, I was the type of person who knocked bitches out on sight.

"I'm gon' fuck this lying bitch up when I see her," I told Ladi as I continued to scroll through the comments from her little entourage.

"She's pregnant, Luv."

"I don't give a fuck. Fuck her and that baby."

"You's a savage, cuz."

After I was done reading the comments and taking a peek at the pictures she had of her and Romeo, to which Romeo wasn't looking in none of the pictures, I handed Ladi back her phone and then ran upstairs to grab mine and called Dagger.

"What?" he answered.

"What? How about your baby momma on Facebook lying, talking about she walked in on us fucking last night," I told him as I paced back and forth in my room.

"She's not lying. She was upstairs the whole time, Luvleigh," he responded.

"Are you fucking kidding me? This bitch talking out her ass on Facebook. I promise you Dagger, I'm knocking her ass out next time I see her. Fuck her, fuck you, and fuck that baby. I put that on my father's grave," I said, hanging up the phone. I texted Hunter.

Me: Do you know where that bitch Berniece live?

While I waited for her to respond, I slipped on my sneakers and started to change purses. I knew her ass knew where she lived. She knew every fucking thing.

My phone rung and it was Hunter. "Yeah, I do. Why? What's up?" she asked.

"I'm going to fuck this bitch up."

"Over Dagger? I can't believe you fucked him and didn't tell me. I should have suspected something. I remembered the way y'all used to feel up on each other and how y'all be eyeing each other at the clubs and shit," she said, annoying the fuck out of me and causing me to roll my eyes.

"Why does everyone think I give a fuck about Dagger, I don't. He and I had sex ten years ago, leave the shit alone. That bitch talking about she smacking me on sight. Well, I wanna see if she 'bout it because you know damn well I am."

"Girl. Pay that girl no mind. She a hating ass bitch, and she's just mad because you whooped that ass the night before. Let that broke bitch talk all the shit she wants. If she ain't saying it to your face, then ain't shit really being said."

"I wanna fight, Hunter. You know I have a short temper. I wanna knock that bitch out, for real for real."

"I know, but she's also pregnant."

"Fuck that baby."

"You are going to hell, sis." She laughed and so did I.

"Alright. I'm about to go back downstairs with Ladi. I'll see you, love."

I hung up the phone, kicked my shoes off, and headed back down the stairs. My phone vibrated, and I thought it was Hunter, but it was Dagger. I opened up the message. It was a picture of BRIKZ with the message: 'y'all think shit funny?'

I responded: Baaaaa!

I think that's what goats say.

Dagger: That's a sheep jack ass.

Me: Well Maaaa! Then nigga. Whatever the fuck a goat says, payback is a motherfucker. Now stop texting my phone.

ONE WEEK LATER

I was sitting on my balcony, with my Kindle and my kush. I had H.E.R playing softly in the background while I was chilling. There was a nice breeze outside that made me think about setting some blankets and shit up here on the balcony and going to sleep. I had on my sexy, royal blue mesh romper that I purchased from Fashion Nova. It had lace trimming and it was see-through, so underneath the bottom I wore a matching royal blue thong. My ass and titties were clearly visible, and I didn't care whatsoever. I was locked in my room alone, so there was no reason to be covered up.

I sat there having a sing-off with myself to H.E.R's song *Free*. I had my feet hanging over one end of the chair, and my head hanging over the other as I took a pull from my blunt.

> *Kissin' me goodnight.*
> *Wakin' up to the sunlight*
> *But you only want me over late*
> *Tall glass of lemonade.*

I continued to sing along to the song, stopping to take a sip of wine. Through the corner of my eye, I thought I seen the hanging azalea bush move. I thought I was tripping, so I sat my glass back down and went back to singing to the music.

"I'm always gon' answer your calls
Talkin' 'bout, "Come and see me-"

I stopped singing when I saw the plant move again. I jumped up from the chair and picked up the first hard thing that was closest to me that would make the biggest impact. I waited to see if the plant moved again, and it did. The weed was really clouding my damn vision. All I could see was a black hoodie with the slasher logo on a hat, come up and I tossed the hot wax from the candle into the person's face before running up and punching him dead in the face.

"Ah shit, Luvleigh, it's me," Dagger shouted as he sat there trying to clear the wax from his face.

"Holy shit, Dagger. What the fuck are you doing here? You don't know how to call?" I stood there getting on him.

"Are you gon' help me get this shit off my face? You almost burned my fucking eye."

"Good. Have ya ass looking like Fetty Wap in this bitch."

I stood there looking at him for a second, trying to decide if I wanted to help him or push his ass over the balcony and into the pool. I walked into my bathroom and wet a washcloth before I brought it back out to him. He cleared his face of the wax and then his nose of the blood that started to leak. "You got a nice little hook on you."

"My bad," I said as I sat back down in my chair. "It's your fault though. What are you doing here?" I asked him. That's when I noticed the bag hooked around his arm. "And what's in the bag?"

He didn't answer, he just sat there as he continued to clean himself up. When he was done, he began to knock shit off of my table.

"Ex-fucking-cuse you, nigga," I uttered, but he ignored my ass. He started taking food platters out of the bag and placed them around the table. Once the bag was empty, he started opening the platters. There were grilled cheese sandwiches, fried hot dogs, white cheddar macaroni and cheese, and French fries with ketchup, hot sauce, and for dessert, fried Oreos. I looked up at him. "Really?" I asked. He nodded his head. This was all of my favorite childhood foods that my daddy used to make us behind my mom's back. She would have had a heart attack if she knew how many times we ate what she called, 'ghetto mess', but we enjoyed the hell out of this shit. "All you missing is su—"

"Sugar water?" he asked, pulling out two white foam cups, a bottle of water and sugar packets.

"Oh my God, I am not drinking that," I jested, covering my mouth.

"Yes, you are," he stated as he started to fix two cups of sugar water. "What? Your taste buds too bougie for this shit?" he asked me.

"For sugar water, yes. I was a kid back then, that shit taste just like colorless Kool-Aid. I'll take my water with no sugar, thank you."

"Shut up and drink the fucking water, Luvleigh. With yo' saddity ass." I gave him the finger.

"How about you kiss, my saddity ass," I said, getting up to go make sure the door was locked. When I stepped back out onto the porch, I caught him eyeing my body in this outfit. "Don't get no fucking ideas, hoe-bag."

He chuckled.

"Hoe-bag, huh? If I'm such a hoe-bag, why you let me hit it? Twice!" he stated, putting up two fingers before he went back to eating a fried hot dog. I picked up one of the spoons and scooped a spoonful of macaroni and cheese into my mouth, while also picking up a fried Oreo, but he slapped my hand. "You don't get dessert until you finish eating."

"Annoying. Why are you here, anyway? You think by you bringing me this delectable grub, that you and I are going to be friends?" I asked him, now picking a grilled cheese triangle and taking a bite.

"Yeah, why, you don't want to be my friend?"

"I don't like your ass."

"I like yours," he responded nonchalantly, making me shake my head and giggle. "I wanted to chill with someone. I couldn't chill with 4Dz because her ass is in the house depressed as fuck, so I came to the only person I would prefer to be around right now," he told me, making me almost smile, but I stopped myself. I didn't want him to know that his words could make me blush, so instead, I just rolled my eyes.

"You always running game. Does that work on all the ladies?" I asked him.

"No, because I don't run game on them. They're not worth my effort. You are," he replied, taking a sip of the sugar water. I made a face indicating that I wasn't impressed by his words.

"You trying to get some pussy?"

"You trying to give me some pussy?" he retorted unenthusiastically.

"Eww, no."

"Fuck you mean, eww? You weren't saying eww when I was eating that pussy."

After he said that, I started thinking back to that night and I caught a chill. It was like I could feel his lips on my pussy, but they weren't. "You know if you want me to do it again, all you have to do is ask."

"Fuck you, I don't want it again. That shit was wack as fuck," I said, standing up and walking into my room to use the bathroom. After using the restroom, I stood looking in the mirror as I washed my hands. Removing my ponytail, I allowed my hair to fall down to my shoulders and started to fluff it. I applied some lip gloss and then walked out the bathroom. I don't know why I just did all that shit like I cared how I looked around him because I didn't. At least I don't think.

When I walked back out onto the balcony, this nigga had the nerve to be sitting there smoking my shit.

"Excuse you. You ain't put in on this, man," I said, taking it from him and sitting back in the chair in the way that I was before he came up here.

"I share my food, but you can't share your bud?" he asked. I rolled my eyes.

"Eat me!"

"You have a potty ass mouth, you know that?"

"Do you know your breath smells like a porta-potty?" I asked jokingly as I looked up, watching my smoke clouds disappear into thin air. He started moving shit around, but I didn't pay any attention to him. That was until my chair started to move and I jumped up quickly.

"Why you so childish?" he asked, as he continued to pull my chair closer and closer to his.

"What are you doing?"

"As told," he replied, swinging my legs around so that they were now in front of him. Spreading my legs, he pulled them, causing the top half of my body to slouch all the way down in the chair so that my back was now in the seat part.

Dagger threw my legs over each shoulder so that my pussy was now at mouth level. He wrapped his big hands around my waist as if he was about to take a bite out of a sandwich. Tugging me closer, he took a nice little nibble of my pussy. Even through this thin ass romper, I could still feel the pressure from his mouth and the heat from his breath. He started to run his tongue across my pussy.

"This shit in the way," he said, moving his hands up my back and then lifting me up so that I was now sitting on his shoulders with my pussy in his face. He stood up and started to walk toward my bedroom as he continued to nibble on my clit. I was too busy watching him, that it never dawned on me to duck once we got closer to the door.

"Ah shit!" I cursed as my head smacked against the door frame.

"Oh shit, you aight?" he asked with a hint of laughter.

"Yeah," I replied, laughing.

"Yo' ass better learn how to duck."

"Shut up, keep it moving," I said slapping him upside his head and he started walking again.

When we got to the bed, he tossed me onto it, causing my hair to cover my entire face. I let it sit there for a few seconds before blowing it out off my face. Dagger had already removed his shirt and was grabbing for my legs and separating them. He crawled onto the bed with his knees until he got between my legs, pushing them up so that my feet were now planted on the bed. His hand moved up and down my lady and then he quickly tore my romper open like my shit was a onesie. I gasped.

"Why would you rip it? I loved this thing," I said as I laid there with my arms folded across my chest and my bottom lip poked out.

"It was cheap anyway," he said in a low voice. "I'll buy you another one, with yo' little spoiled ass," he said, smacking me in the face hard, but not that hard. I went to smack him back, but he pinned my arms back and against the bed with one arm, before he started fumbling with my thong with the other hand. He placed his lips onto mine and we kissed for what felt like forever. That was until he unlatched his mouth from mine and was kissing down my body. He stopped at my right titty, biting my nipple through the fabric of the lace romper. Once again, his savage ass decided to tear the strap of the romper, removing my titty and taking it into his mouth.

"You know I could have just took my arm out the strap, right?"

"Mmhh," he answered. The feeling of his tongue flicking across my nipple sent chills up my spine. He sat up and then ripped the other side, pulling my left titty out and doing the same thing he did to the right. I grabbed on to this head as it moved in circular motions over my breast, making my nipple as hard as chocolate chips.

After some time, he rolled over onto his back and was pulling me on top of him. I was about to straddle him, but he instructed me to stand.

"What are you doing?" I asked him.

"I want you to sit on my face," he told me.

"What?"

"You heard me. Come here," he ordered, taking me by the hand and helping me to stand. I was standing over his face looking down at him as he bit down on those sexy lips. He was just sitting there, waiting for me to put my pussy on his face. I lowered myself down onto his face, and he wrapped his arms around my thighs and went to work. His tongue traveled up and down the slit of my pussy, causing me to quiver with excitement. I found myself running from his lethal ass tongue, but he would grip my thighs tighter, making me stay still and take the licking. After about another minute, I reached down, entangling my fingers in his hair as I started to ride his face.

My body shook as my long overdue orgasm started to take over my body. I let go of his hair and I remained on top of his face as he continued to tickle my clit. My body was Harlem-shaking on his face until he finally let me go, and I fell onto the bed on my back. I was now laying between his legs with my own sitting on top of his shoulder.

"Damn, I thought yo' ass got electrocuted," he jested.

"Screw you," I replied.

"Ok." He pulled himself from under me and sat up on his knees. Lowering his black Nike sweat shorts, his dick sprung out, already standing at attention. The tip of it glistened with pre-cum.

"You are not putting that thing in me," I told him.

"Why not?" he asked, peering down at me as he continued to remove his shorts. Once they were completely off, he hovered over me, placing his face into the crook of my neck, and planting soft kisses there, sending sparks up and down my spine.

"Because you not getting me pregnant with that pre-cum oozing out your hole."

He started laughing and then he sat up on his knees, with the sexiest grin on his face. Grabbing onto his dick, he jerked it slowly as he peered down at me. "What this?" he asked, brushing his thumb over the tip, getting some of the pre-cum on his finger. "It's a really small chance of you getting pregnant from this," he said, and then wiped it on my forehead. I smacked his hand away and chuckled lightly.

"Why would you do that? Nasty ass. You acting like teenage-you, right now," I told him as I wiped at my forehead.

"You loved teenage me. That's why you use to let me feel on you and pop that cherry," he whispered as he came closer to my ear.

As he nibbled on my ear, I could feel his dick daggering at my opening.

"Oh God," I moaned, throwing my head back into the bed. Once he had all of himself snuggled deep inside of me, he pulled it in and out of me, slowly, until my body started to relax, and he picked up his speed. With every thrust he delivered, I could feel myself becoming wetter.

"You know this pussy is mine forever, right?" he spoke into my ear. I shook my head 'no' and he pushed into me harder. "This shit is mine, Luvleigh, you hear me?" When I didn't answer, he pushed into me harder, making me moan out loud. He placed one hand over my mouth and the other, he eased it under my back, wrapping it around my waist. In one swift motion, he rolled over, rolling me on top of him. I tried to sit up, but he held my body down as he began jackhammering my pussy, which sent my body into overdrive. The smacking of our skin echoed throughout the room, and at this point, I didn't care if anyone heard us. Every time he pulled his dick out, my pussy juices came through dripping. His hand remained over my mouth as he continued to fuck me up.

I had about three orgasms in about fifteen minutes from this one position. I was spent and ready to roll over and put my thumb in my mouth, but he was not having that shit. He was not quitting until he made me say that this pussy was his. I gave in and told him exactly what he wanted to hear, just so he could show my pussy some mercy, but nope.

"If you let anyone touch this pussy that ain't me, I promise you, I will kill them and then kill you. You hear me?" he asked, and I nodded my head up and down. I had to admit, I was liking all this psycho talk. "I told you when we were younger, that you were going to get used to seeing my dick, didn't I?" Once again, with my head buried deep into the crook of his neck, I nodded it up and down as I continued to take this thrashing. Every now and then I would bite down on his neck. "Why did I tell you that?" he asked. I thought back to the conversation we had that day in the bathroom. I didn't have to think too hard because I thought about that day almost every day.

"Because, I was gon' be married to it," I replied, laughing as I thought about how many times he told me we were going to get married.

"That's right. This my shit," he stated, rolling me back over onto my back as he continued to work on his nut.

STAR

*S*un and I were on our way back home from the studio. I was dropping this nigga off at home so that I could skate the fuck off to Hunter's house to get my balls played with. I would be on my way there now if I didn't have to drive this fucker every damn where. This nigga got popped with a DUI and DWI, three fucking times. This nigga will never fucking learn. He was my brother though, and I would do any fucking thing for him, my mother, and my sister. I was the oldest, so I had to protect the family. Do what my father couldn't at this point.

I was pissed the fuck off after hearing that my sister fucked that nigga, Dagger. That was like a fucking *dagger* to my fucking heart. She admitted that it happened years back when my father was still around, and we were all cool with the niggas, but we ain't anymore. Now that shit is like sleeping with the fucking enemy, and I wasn't gon' have that shit. I would dead that nigga before I let him touch my fucking sister again.

"These fucking burgers are hitting, nigga," Sun spoke with a mouth full of White Castle burgers.

"Nigga, you think I can't fucking tell. Yo' ass been farting up my fucking whip, nigga. How the fuck am I going to get pussy in this bitch, with it smelling like yo' ass?"

"What pussy you getting in this shit? We can barely move in this bitch," he asked, talking about my new Bugatti. He was right, it was a little tight with the both of us in this bitch. I doubt if I would be able to smash a bitch in here. "And Hunter got a place, why would you want to hit it in the car?"

"I wasn't talking about Hunter. I'm talking about another bitch that I might meet and need to hit real quick."

He nodded his head up and down, signaling that he understood. I'm sure that he did. Pussy was being thrown at my brother and I, on a daily. They knew we had money, and you'd be surprised how quick bitches lose their morals and self-respect for money. I guess we have Cardi B to thank for that. We had bitches offering to let my brother and I dub 'em. You think we ain't take that bitch up on her offer. We did and called that bitch an Uber once we were done with her.

Hunter was wifey though, and she knew it, so she never tripped when bitches are throwing themselves into my lap. But don't let them get too ballsy. My baby will start throwing bows with no problem.

We were like three blocks from our crib. I thought I was tripping when I noticed a car similar to that nigga, Dagger. I looked at it and continued to drive, thinking maybe someone had the same shit as him. But then I realized that I drove up and down this block every fucking day and had never seen a car like that until tonight.

"Hold up," I said, busting a U-turn in the middle of the block, almost causing an accident. I pulled up next to the car and got out. Turning the flashlight on my iPhone on, I began to look inside the car. Once I noticed the vice grips that this nigga has been carrying around since we were younger, I knew that this was his car. Shutting the flashlight off, I backed up from the car and started looking around at the houses. I knew mostly everyone who lived in the area, and I knew for sure he wouldn't be seeing anyone over here. It was only old white people who lived in this neighborhood. I walked back to the driver's side and reached under the seat, pulling out my pistol. I checked to make sure that this shit was loaded before I placed it into my lap. Sun did the same thing.

"You think them niggas at the house?' he asked.

"I don't know, but we are about to fucking find out."

I busted another reckless U-turn and sped to my house. I pressed the code into the front gate and it opened. I sped up to the house and we attempted to jump out on some bad boy shit, but with this little ass fucking car, we had to ease our way out. I set my gun on top of the car, and then I grabbed onto the top of the car so that I could pull the rest of my body out. Once I was out, I walked around to help this nigga out.

"That's all them fucking cheeseburgers you just ate," I told him, as he finally climbed out completely.

"Nigga, you need to get rid of this little ass fucking car. This the last time I get my ass in that bitch."

"Shut up," I told him as we trekked to the house. He was right though. I was getting my ass a damn truck tomorrow.

We walked into the house, checking the first floor. Everything appeared to be in order, but that didn't mean those fucking Masters weren't in this bitch somewhere. We headed straight up the stairs. Our Timbs stomped up the steps as we took them shits two at a time. We stopped at my mother's room first, and I knocked on the door before walking in. She was sitting at her vanity, putting on her night cream.

"Hello, children," she greeted us. "What's going on?" she asked as she wiped her hands onto the towel.

"Everything cool here?" Sun asked.

"Yeah, why wouldn't it be?"

"We saw that nigga, Dagger's car, parked around the corner. We thought those niggas were up to some shit."

She sat there for a minute before jumping to her feet immediately, grabbing a skeleton key off the dresser. She brushed passed us as she walked further down the hall toward Luvleigh's room that was at the end of the hallway.

My mother placed her ear to the door first before attempting to place the key into the key slot. Her hands were shaking for some reason. Once she had the key in the door, she pushed it open.

The room was dark, but the light from the hallway had lit the room up, and we were able to clearly see Luvleigh lying in the bed. My mother quietly stepped into the room and up to her bed. She then walked into the middle of the room where she just stood there. I didn't know what she was doing.

She came back over to the door and shut it behind her.

"Everything is fine boys. I'm going to bed," she said as she walked back to her room. Sun and I looked at each other, and then tucked our guns back into our pants.

"Sis was smoking some fire shit," Sun mentioned.

"Hell yeah. I smelled that shit as soon as the door opened. She been holding out on us," I added. Sun went into his room, but I went back out to my car. I climbed in and drove back to where Dagger's car was, but it was gone. Some shit was up, and I was going to figure it out.

JULIET

*J*got back in my room and sat back at my vanity. Under this face mask, the thick vein in my forehead was protruding and pulsating. On top of the smell of weed, I can smell the remnants of a man's cologne. To know that she had the audacity to bring that man inside of my home had me infuriated. I was going to make sure this shit never happened again. I pushed the mirror of my vanity and it popped open. The light inside of the safe automatically came on, revealing the Desert Eagle, the dagger, and the valves of cyanide, spider venom, and belladonna. I brushed my hand across them all, stopping at the gun, and I removed it from its holder. It was my husband's gun. I would like to think that me and this gun had some things in common. It was a beautiful and deadly piece of metal, much like myself.

After admiring the gun, I placed it back inside the safe and shut it. I strolled over to my bed and grabbed my cell phone before flopping onto my bed. I dialed a number and waited for it to ring.

"Hey baby, it's Queen. I need a favor... I need someone eliminated, that means I need you. Can you help me with that?"

THREE WEEKS LATER

LUVLEIGH

*A*fter busting down some major cash on Fifth Avenue in Manhattan, Ladi, Hunter, and I sat down at Benihana's, replenishing our energy with some sushi and cocktails. We still had to hit Chanel and Burberry, and Hunter wanted to go into UGGs for some odd reason. It was freaking spring, she wasn't going to need UGGs no time soon, but the way this weather is set up, you never know. I could shop until I freaking dropped. We had already been in Saks for like three hours, Barneys for about two hours, and Louis Vuitton for another two hours, and of course I wanted to get my Nicki Minaj on, so I copped me some Fendi prints.

I had already blown through about fifteen thousand, and these two bitches weren't too far behind me. I don't know what Hunter was doing, but my brother was dropping stacks in her pocketbook and Ladi's ol' secretive ass, was getting money from somebody but she wasn't telling us. Whoever it was, was balling because cuzzo had stacks.

I set my phone down on the table as I picked up my coconut mojito, and sipped from it, making a face.

"Zammmnnn, that's strong but good as hell," I said, placing the glass back down. My cell phone vibrated, and I picked it up, smiling at the text message and then closed it out.

"Who the fuck you been texting this whole time?" Hunter asked, as she side-eyed me. I didn't answer, I just sipped my drink.

"Whoever the fuck it is, must be slamming that dick down good because this bitch smiles every time that phone vibrates," Ladi added. I still ignored them both because if they knew who it was, they would start with all the judging, and I wasn't beat for all that shit.

"Spill it, bitch."

I shook my head and responded, "Nope."

"It's Dagger," Ladi assumed.

"Eww, no it's not."

"Who else would it be?" Ladi asked, causing me to form a frown.

"What you mean who else can it be? What you trying to say, I can't get a nigga other than Dagger? There's plenty of niggas chasing this cat."

"Name one," Hunter said.

"Tr8z," I responded. Hunter rolled her eyes and I noticed Ladi tense up for a second before picking up her drink.

"So you're fucking Tr8z?" Hunter asked. "You letting him stick that ding-a-ling in that chicken wing?" she asked, doing some kind of thrusting dance.

"Chicken wing? That's what we calling it now?"

"It rhymes, shit."

I shook my head and laughed. "He's not sticking nothing inside of me. He ate my cooch once and I was told that he has the gift that keeps on giving, if you know what I mean."

Once I said that, Ladi spit out her drink while Hunter's dramatic ass jumped up out her chair and started doing some kind of shouting dance.

"Aren't you glad you ain't let that nigga hit?" Hunter asked.

"More than, girl. He texts me every now and then, trying to get up, but I'm just not beat for that shit. He can keep his herpes all to himself. Crazy part is that I found this out after I let him put his mouth on my shit. I took my ass to the doctor immediately. When I got the all clear from the doctor, I said never again. Now we text back and forth, and he let me listen to his music. That's it."

"Damn, cheers to a close-damn-call, bitch," Hunter said, putting her drink up and I did mine. We looked over at the now quiet Ladi as she put her drink up next to ours and clinked.

After we ate our sushi and ordered another round of drinks, we left out the restaurant and walked back down to do some more shopping.

Another 5,000 dollars later, and we were jumping into my new 2018 blacked out Porsche Macan GTS. I thought about getting it painted purple like I did my Cayenne, but this black just looked so sexy, I couldn't ruin it.

As we were pulling out the garage, I spotted Berniece hugged up with a man. I pulled over and tugged out my phone, taking pictures.

"Look at this bitch," I said, getting their attention. They both looked out of the window.

"That bitch is such a hoe," Hunter said.

"Fo sho," Ladi added. "Why you taking pictures?"

"So I can show them to Dagger," I answered.

"Why do you care if you not fucking him?" Hunter inquired.

"Because I wanna ruin this bitch's life. Her ass keeps talking shit about me on Facebook, and I can't smack her ass, so. All she has to throw in people's face is how Dagger is taking care of her and how she's wifey. I wonder if he's going to continue to take care of her, once he starts second-guessing if that baby is his. That's if she's really pregnant. Shouldn't her ass be showing already?" I asked, sounding like a hater, but I was far from that.

"Not really, some people don't start showing until their fifth month."

After I had all the pictures I needed, I waited until she pulled off and I followed every turn she made, making sure to stay a few cars behind.

"Are we really doing this?" Ladi's ass asked from the back seat. Since we left Benihana's, she's been quiet and had a slight attitude.

"You wanna get out? I can leave you right here on the George

Washington bridge," I told her, looking in the rearview mirror at her as she looked out the window. She didn't respond. "What's wrong with you, woman? You been quiet since we left the restaurant."

"Nothing, I'm chilling," she responded, unenthusiastically.

I was going to continue to question her, but I decided I would just leave her alone.

I followed Berniece all the way to Dagger's house. I thought she was going to lead me back to the house of the dude she was in the car with, but nope. She gave me something better.

The two of them got out her car and walked around the front of it, where they engaged in another kiss.

"I know damn well she is not about to bring that nigga in Dagger's house," Hunter asked, as we both sat up to get a closer look. I started snapping pictures of them walking inside the house.

"Alright, can we go now?" Ladi asked. I looked back at her.

"Nope. Come on, Hunter," I said, tapping her on the legs, and like the down ass bitch she was, she hopped out right along with me.

We both crept around the side of the house. We peeked through the window which gave us a clear view of the living room. Berniece and this dude sat on Dagger's couch, slobbing each other down.

"Where the fuck is Dagger?" Hunter asked.

"He's been staying at his father's house," I answered, knowing I was about to get the third fucking degree.

"And how the hell you know that?" she whispered.

"I just do. Now focus."

"Will you take the picture, so we can go."

"Nah, I want to wait until I see some fucking."

We sat there a little longer, peeping through the window. I knew Ladi was getting mad while waiting on us in the car, but oh well. This shit was fun. She should have gotten her ass out of the car and came with us.

Our waiting paid off when Berniece dropped down to her knees and began to suck the nigga off. My mouth dropped open at the same time that I pressed record on my phone. This bitch had bomb ass head skills. She was sucking, slurping, and spitting. It was gross, but at the same time, fascinating at how bomb her skills were.

She was just getting into it when the sound of someone sleeping on their horn went off. "What the fuck?" I asked as we both ducked down, and I ended the video. I peeked back through the window to see that Berniece had stopped her savage assault on the dick. She looked toward the door, and then her head suddenly looked toward the window, and I quickly ducked back down.

"Abort the mission, bitch," I whispered to Hunter and we both took off running down the driveway with our heels click-clacking against the cobblestone. We got to the car, and come to find out, it was fucking Ladi pressing on the horn. When we got inside, she stopped and was now in the backseat having the laugh of her life.

"Bitch, what the fuck? It was just getting good," I told her as I started the car and bust a U-turn before speeding off down the block.

Ladi still hadn't stopped laughing.

"Bitch, ain't shit funny, I almost broke my fucking neck running in these heels," Hunter told her.

"No bitch, you almost got knocked-out by your own fucking titties running like that," Ladi said, through laughter. I sat there for a second and then I started laughing because as we were running, I could see her titties bouncing up and down from the corner of my eyes.

"I thought Luv was gon' have to drag yo' ass the rest of the way down the driveway once your titties KO'd yo' ass."

We all joined in the laugh this time. I don't know if Berniece seen us and quite frankly, I didn't give a damn. She may not have saw us, but we saw her, and Dagger was gon' see this shit too.

AFTER DROPPING the two of them off, I rushed home and started to unpack all of my many bags. When I got in, my mother was sitting on the couch. I was surprised she didn't follow me up the stairs once she had seen all the designer bags I had in my hand. She really hasn't said much to me in the last three weeks. I couldn't take her bitterness much longer, so I hired a realtor to look for my very own place. So far, the places she's been showing me have either been way too big or too small for me. I told her I needed a closet about the size of a studio apartment for all the shit I had, and I had to have a garage for my car. Although I had the money to get my own house, I wasn't ready for that just yet. I was still young. A nice two bedroom with a walk-in closet, in a gated community with a security guard controlling access to the property, was good enough for me.

I took a quick shower and laid down in the bed until it was time for me to go out. Before laying down, I made sure to lock my door because I was tired of waking up to Juliet's creepy ass staring down at me with those feline eyes.

I hadn't sent the pictures to Dagger yet, I figured I would wait until later. Right now, I needed a quick nap.

Two hours later, I was being awakened by my phone's alarm. I turned it off and started to get dressed in a gray spandex skirt, a coral crop top, and a pair of white, coral, and navy-blue air max. I grabbed my car keys, my cell phone, and wallet before slowly and quietly sneaking out of the house, making sure that I wasn't being followed.

Within twenty minutes I was pulling up to Dahnert's Lake. I parked directly behind his Lamborghini. I grabbed my phone and walked through the dark park, using my phone's flashlight to guide me around the track where I found Dagger sitting on a bench with his phone in his hand. From what I could see, we were the only ones here.

He must've heard me coming because I tend to drag my feet when I walk. He glanced my way and then stood up. When he stood up, I ran and jumped into his arms and kissed him like I missed him. Like I hadn't seen him in weeks when in fact, I've been seeing him almost every day for the past two weeks. I don't know what happened after that night we had sex, but that entire week after, thoughts of him invaded my mind nonstop. When he admitted that he couldn't stop thinking about me as well, we met up at his carwash that night, where we had sex over and over again.

We had sex any and everywhere we could get it in at. There was the car wash, inside the movie theater, the bathroom of the club, our cars, now the park. I think this was another reason why I wanted to get my own place as well. There was no way we could go to either one of our homes.

"What's up?" he asked as he held me tightly.

"You," I answered, wrapping my arms around his neck. He kissed my lips before we walked back over to the bench and sat down, with me in his lap.

"You know we can't keep sneaking around like this, right? Eventually, we are going to have to tell those crazy people we call family," he said, stretching his arms across the bench.

"But why? This is so fun," I whined, making a pouty face.

"You enjoy this shit? Sneaking the fuck around like we're teenagers, Luvleigh?" he asked sternly.

"No, but it makes the sex so much more exciting." I laughed.

"This shit turns your little ass on?" he asked, biting down on his bottom lip. That shit was so sexy and had my juices flowing like a leaky faucet.

"We don't have to tell them. We can just run away to Mexico or something."

"Mexico? You do know people run away from Mexico every day to come here. Shouldn't that tell you something?"

"You right. What about the Bahamas?"

"I can get with the Bahamas." We both shared a laugh before kissing again. "Shit, while we're at it, we might as well go down to the city hall and get married then. I always told you I was going to marry you when we were younger."

"You sure did."

"Yo' ass told me I was going to be a hoe until the day my dick fell off or I dropped dead," he said, making me laugh. "So do you think I've changed?"

"I'll admit that I was wrong back then. You have changed... kinda."

"So let's go get married."

"Alright. Let's do it."

"You don't waste no time, huh?" he said, unbuttoning his Louis Vuitton belt. I started to giggle.

"No, I meant let's go get married," I told him, laughing at his silliness.

"Tomorrow morning?"

"Ok," I agreed, not thinking much about it. "Now, can we get down to fucking and stop all this chit-chatting and shit."

He smiled and then kissed my lips as he opened his jeans. I was ready for this shit, I made sure not to put on any panties for easy access. He pulled out his dick and was about to lower me down onto it, but I stopped.

"What happened?" he asked.

"I want to try something," I told him as I climbed off of his lap and squatted down in front of him.

"Ah shit!" he said excitedly. I took a deep breath as I grabbed his dick. I tried to play back what I had witnessed Berniece do earlier today. I covered his erect dick with my mouth, getting it wet.

"Mmm," he moaned. *Ah shit, good start, Luv,* I thought to myself as I came up and smiled to myself in the dark. I released some spit from my mouth onto his dick, which truly grossed me out, but I went with it. "Oh shit, where you learned that from?" he asked me, but I didn't respond. *I feel like a pro already,* I praised myself as I covered his dick with my mouth again and started to bob my head up and down. *Yeah, buddy. This isn't as bad as I thought...* "Ahhh shit!" he yelped, this time in a painful cry than a satisfying moan. *Oh damn, I fucked up!* I panicked and released his dick from my mouth.

"What did I do?" I asked him, backing away.

"Teeth, baby. No teeth. Come up here, we'll work on that later. It was a nice try though," he said with a hint of laughter, making me laugh as well.

I stood over him and slowly straddled his lap, inserting his dick inside of my warm pussy pocket. Since the time we had sex at his house, I couldn't get enough of him. I can see why that bitch Berniece was so crazy over this nigga. The way he stretched my walls out, was the best feeling in the world. You would have thought that I was a professional fucker, but I wasn't. Technically, I was still a beginner, but I was slowly becoming a professional when it came to taking dick from Dagger.

"Mmmm," I moaned, biting down on my bottom lip as I started to rotate my hips the way Dagger taught me, taking every inch of him inside me. His hands gripped my waist as he guided me up and down and round.

I could feel Dagger pushing himself deeper inside of me as I rode him.

"That's right, baby girl, take all this dick," he told me, and I did as he asked, bouncing up and down harder. I could feel my juices drenching his thighs. The sound of our skin smacking together could be heard, but it wasn't as loud because we were outside.

Dagger stood up from the bench and turned around. He placed my feet on the ground and then turned me around, directing me to kneel on the bench. After sliding that dick back inside me, he started pounding my ass out. I leaned over the bench, throwing my ass back, meeting his thrust.

I turned my head to look back at it like Trina said in her song, and I caught a glimpse of a light. It was someone walking toward us.

"Oh shit! Someone's coming," I told him, never stopping as I continued to throw my ass back.

"So," he answered. I swear that was his favorite fucking word. He talked about me, but I think the thrill of almost getting caught, turned his ass on just as much as it did me. "I'm almost there," he said in a breathy voice. I could tell he was about to nut by how tight his grip was on my waist. He placed his foot up on the bench as I sat there watching the light get closer and closer. If Dagger wasn't worried about it, I wasn't going to worry about it either.

"I'm about to nut, Luv," he warned. "In or out?" he asked.

"Out," I told him.

"I thought we were getting married, so it shouldn't matter."

"We ain't married yet, so shut up and pull out," I told him. He started thrusting harder and harder until I felt him pull back. I turned around. I couldn't see because it was dark, but I knew he was standing there, jerking the rest of the nut out of his shaft.

Once he was done, he pulled up his pants and grabbed my hand as we started running the opposite way of the oncoming light. My skirt was still above my waist, so my ass was out.

"I wonder if they saw us?" I asked.

"I doubt it," he answered as he gently tugged me through the playground, up the hill, and to our vehicles. I pulled my skirt down as he pushed me against my truck and we began to engage in a passionate kiss that I never wanted to end. Every time he pulled back I would pull him in for another kiss, and when I pulled back, he pushed forward, taking my lips between his.

"What time do you want to meet up at the City Hall?" he asked.

"You dead serious?" I asked him.

"Yeah, I'm dead ass serious. Why, you're not?"

"I don't even like you. In fact, I'm supposed to be hating you right now, how are we about to get married?"

"A lot of couples don't like each other, but they love each other. Love is all we need."

"Oh my God! I can't believe I'm about to do this," I said as I slapped my hands softly against my cheeks in disbelief.

"We don't have to," he ensured me, squeezing my arms. I sat there thinking for a minute. *Was I ready to be with someone for the rest of my life?* I knew I enjoyed being around him and seeing him, and I knew I didn't want that to stop. I have grown to love Dagger in this small amount of time we've been sneaking around. He made me feel safe, he made me feel like I was a grown woman. He made me feel free. *Fuck it! I like new and exciting things, and this was one of them. I also enjoyed pissing my mother off and I knew her ass was going to die once she found out.*

"Let's do it," I concluded, wrapping my arms around his neck.

"Alright. See you tomorrow, soon to be Mrs. Masters."

"Oh my God, that just sounds so weird."

"Get used to it," he said, kissing me before walking me around to the driver's side. He opened my door and I climbed inside. We kissed once again before he closed my door. I pushed to start my car and pulled off. I looked into the rearview mirror at him as he waved at me.

I smiled and continued to drive home. My phone vibrated, and I glanced down at it while still trying to concentrate on the road. It was a text message.

Dagger: *You're going to need a witness. I suggest you choose someone quick.*

Damn, I forgot about that. But who can I ask? Hunter or Ladi?

DAGGER

*A*fter I got home, I sat in the living room, doing some research on marriage laws in New Jersey. Come to find out, we had to sign a marriage certificate and had to wait seventy-two hours before we could officially get married. That shit was way too long. Tomorrow, I was going to contact my personal lawyer and see how I could speed this shit up. On a positive note, this gave me time to plan something more memorable. Luvleigh deserved better than a City Hall marriage. I knew this shit seemed a little rushed, but I loved her, and I told Luvleigh when we were younger that we were going to get married. She never believed me. On top of that, I wanted to get her away from that family. Especially her mother. She was controlling, conniving, and from the shit my father was telling me, she's vindictive and murderous.

From the time Luvleigh walked into the club with that baby blue dress, which stuck to her figure like a second layer of skin, I couldn't stop thinking about her little ass. I played the 'I don't give a fuck card' well, but it was all a front. The sight of her had triggered feelings I felt for her back when we younger. When I walked into the restaurant and saw her kissing homeboy, that shit pissed me off completely, and I knew it should have been me that she was kissing up on.

This shit was about to shock everyone, but I hadn't planned on telling anyone until afterward. However, there was one person I had to tell before.

I pulled myself from off of the couch and went upstairs. I made a stop at my temporary room to grab something before going into 4Dz' room. Before I knocked on her door, I placed my ear to it and I heard DRS's song *Gangsta Lean* playing. I shook my head and knocked on the door. She opened it, looking depressed as shit. Her hair hadn't been done in weeks, and she hadn't bothered to get dressed, so she'd been walking around in a tank top, boxers, and some thick ass socks pulled halfway up her calves. Her eyes were puffy, and her nose was snotty.

"Seriously, nigga?" I asked, shutting her bedroom door behind me as I followed behind her while she dragged her feet back over to the bed. "Yo' ass still tripping over them damn fake dicks?"

"Man, fuck you. You don't understand," she lamented, standing up from the bed. I held in my laughter.

"Alright, alright. You right, I don't understand. I have something for you," I said, pulling a gift-wrapped box from behind my back. I handed it to her.

"What is this?" she asked, sniveling.

"Open it," I told her. She looked over the box before she started to unwrap it. "Now, I know it's not going to replace the ones you had, but it's a start. Maybe it'll help you get back to your normal self again." She finished unwrapping the box and looked it over.

"You got me a new dick, man?"

"Yeah. I mean, it's like a starter dick until you can start your collection over again. I know you've been too depressed to go outside and shit; I figured this one would get you started."

"Thanks, man. I appreciate this shit. I could have bought my own, but I couldn't bear to go outside without my dicks. I feel naked, and like a girl without them."

"No problem, cuz. Yo. I need a favor from you," I told her.

"What you need, nigga?"

"I need you to be a witness at my wedding."

"What the fuck!" she shouted. "How fucking long have I been locked up in this bitch? When did this shit happen? I know you ain't marrying that hoe, Berniece. Yo, listen to me. Listen to your favorite cousin, your best fucking friend, just because that bitch is pregnant, doesn't mean you have to marry the hoe."

"Nigga, sit down. It ain't Berniece."

"Oh, good. Who is it then? A new bitch? She must be popping to get you to marry her ass this quick."

"It's Luvleigh."

After I revealed the name, she started to laugh sporadically. I guess she was waiting for me to say 'psych' or 'nah, I'm just playing', but when it never came, she smacked my ass upside the head.

"Are you out of your fucking mind?" she asked, followed by another smack to the back of my head.

"Nigga, you know how I feel about her. How I always felt about her."

"I thought that shit passed once we got older and started hating the Carters."

"I do hate the Carters, but I love Luvleigh, and I know this marriage is going to hurt the Carters to their core once they find out I've turned one of them into one of us."

"Are you sure about this? Are you sure you want to get married for the right reason, or is this just another way to fuck with the Carters?" 4Dz asked.

"Nah, it's for the right reason. We've seen each other every day for the past three weeks, and I enjoy the time I've been spending with her ass. Not just the fucking, but the conversations we have, her life plans, the way she thinks, the feelings I get when she's next to me, and the fact that I never want her to leave."

"Damn, sounds like you got it bad for a Carter. Ain't that some shit. You do know this is going to start an all-out war, right? Have you told Unc?"

"Not until after. You're the only one I've told so far."

"Damn. I mean, I'll be honored, nigga. I know you don't do shit without thinking it through, so I trust you know what you're doing," she said. "Shit, I gotta get my hair done. Can I go like this?" she asked, pointing to her hair and then down to the clothes she was wearing.

"No, nigga. Go get that nappy ass head done and find something decent to wear. It's my motherfucking wedding. You have three days though, so you can still rock this for another two days."

She stood up from the bed at the same time that I did and held out her hand. "Congratu-fucking-lations, nigga," she said, shaking my hand. I thanked her and then left out of her room.

I went back to my room and took a quick shower. When I was done, I laid back on the bed and started texting Luvleigh, letting her know that we had to wait seventy-two hours, and that we needed to fill out a marriage application. She agreed, and then said she had something to show me. I immediately got excited thinking she was sending me a naked picture or something. When the video came in, it was of Berniece sucking that producer nigga's dick. I ain't give a fuck about her sucking the nigga's dick, it just pissed me off that her disrespectful ass was doing it at my place. My blood started to boil. That hoe had to get the fuck out of my house.

I put my phone down, but picked it back up immediately when it vibrated, thinking that it was Luvleigh, but it wasn't.

"Yo," I answered.

"Oh my God, where have you been all my life?" she responded, making me laugh.

"What's going on, Max? I haven't heard from you in while."

"I know. Hubby started getting suspicious, I thought I would fall back for a while, but I'm missing you. Can you hook me up? I need my fix. I have an itch that only you can scratch."

"As tempting as it sounds, Max, I can't. I found me a girl, and I'm in love with her."

"Oh my God, really D? That's good…Wait, hold up, it's not that crazy chick that's been playing on my phone, right?" she inquired. I shook my head and chuckled.

"Nah, it's not. It's a childhood friend who I've reconnected with. She's great."

"Good, good, I'm happy for you," she said in a low tone.

"Are you really?"

"Not really, that means I either have to find some new dick or deal with the weak shit I have at home. You sure you can't come see me one last time," she begged.

"Nah, baby, I can't. I'll get at you though. I have some things I have to handle."

"Ok. Goodbye, D."

I hung up the phone and shook my head. I was really about to be a one-woman man.

JULIET

$\mathcal{I}$ laid on my bed, butt-ass-naked. I had some soft music playing, the lights dimmed, and candles lit. I was oiled down in my Avon Skin So Soft body oil. My naked body was dripped in some of the finest diamonds. There was a light knock on the door, and then it opened as Cream came walking in with his fine ass.

"Hello, handsome," I greeted him.

"Hello, Mrs. Carter. You waiting for me?" he asked.

"Am I? You're right on time."

"Good," he said, walking over to the bed and pulling me by my ankles. He turned me over and lifted me on all fours. Spreading my legs, he dove in head first as he started to eat my pussy, sucking it dry, and then moistening it back up with his spit. Every now and then he would stick his tongue inside of my asshole, and I would back my ass back on to it because it felt so good.

He pulled his tongue out and went back to eating my pussy.

"Mmmm, Cream, baby, that feels so good. You are filled with many talents, baby," I told him as I continued to moisten his face with my pussy juices. "What did you find out for me?" I asked him. He stopped eating my pussy before standing up behind me, removing his shirt and unbuttoning his pants.

"She met up with him again," he responded, pushing his dick inside of me.

"Oh yes, baby. Just like that," I told him as he roughly slammed into me, and then pulled himself out, only to enter me again. "Did she fuck him?" I asked.

"Yes, right there in the park, Mama. If you asked me, them two are in love."

Listening to him say my daughter was in love with a Masters had pissed me off, but not enough to stop me from fucking. I had to put a stop to this shit as soon as possible. Every time Luvleigh called herself sneaking out of the house, I had Cream follow her to find out where she was going, and each time, she was meeting up with Dagger. I told her to leave him alone, she chose to defy me, so I had to teach her a little lesson.

"Fuck me harder," I demanded, backing my ass back into him. Just as I instructed, he started fucking me harder, but not hard enough. "Harder!" I yelled, and once again, he picked up the pace, as well as his aggression level.

"Yes, just like that."

The sound of our skin smacking echoed throughout the room, and I didn't care if anyone heard us. He flipped me over onto my back and pulled my body to the edge of the bed. He rammed his dick inside of me, holding on to my waist. I could see my juices as they dripped down his leg. It turned me on even more.

"I'm about to nut, baby," he said as he bent down and took one of my titties into his mouth.

"Already?"

"You got the pussy of a twenty-year-old. This shit so fucking tight, and wet, and you're so fucking beautiful, I can't help it. I'll get it back up, I promise."

He stood back up and grabbed my waist tighter, digging in deeper and deeper before he started to slow down until he came to a complete stop. He stood there nutting inside of me. When he was done, he collapsed on top of me as I laid there, stroking his sweaty head. Once he gained the strength, he pulled himself off of me and laid next to me.

"You are amazing, Juliet."

"I know. Do you love me?" I asked him.

"Of course, I do."

"Would you do anything for me?"

"Anything as long as you keep letting me inside this pussy," he answered, standing back up and pushing me further on the bed as he laid between my legs, spreading them, and began licking at my pussy.

"I need you to do me a really big favor. If you do this for me, you can have me whenever, however, as long as you want. I'll even pay you. How does that sound?" I asked him as I sat up and pushed him onto his back. I climbed over him and gripped his semi-hard dick before I started to ease it inside of me.

"I'll do anything for you, Juliet."

"Ok. It involves Luvleigh," I said as I slowly started to move up and down until his dick bricked up, and I was able to get a good bounce going.

ROMEO

I gazed up at the ceiling as I laid in my bed, receiving head from some chick I paid. I couldn't feel shit. Dagger was right, my shit was a soggy ass fucking noddle that couldn't even get hard anymore. The last time my dick was hard, was ten years ago when X caught me in the bedroom fucking Juliet. She was my last fuck, and boy was it good until we were interrupted. I don't know what it was about that woman that made me do everything she ever asked me to do. The only reason why I still had hope that my dick could get hard, was because whenever I saw Juliet, I would feel a surge of energy go through my dick. Which gave me the hope that I could still get my fuck on again, one day. I was starting to come to the realization that maybe it was just the person. But I knew I would never stick my dick in that poisonous woman again.

Back when I was fucking her, I would have done anything for her. After I got shot and X kicked her ass out, she was at my bedside every single day. X knew it, but she didn't know that he did. They served her divorce papers while she was in my hospital room. She ripped them up in front of me and left. She never came back.

She refused to divorce X. She knew that if she signed those divorce papers, that she would get nothing, and everything would go to

Luvleigh, not her or the twins. I think once X found us fucking, he came to the realization that Star and Sun, weren't his, and they weren't. They were, in fact, mine. I knew it, Juliet knew it, but she refused to believe it. The twin gene ran in my family hard. I was a twin. My boys, Aries and Leo were twins. If you put Aries and Leo next to Star and Sun, you would have thought they were quadruplets. X wasn't a stupid nigga, in fact, he was one of the smartest niggas I knew. Yeah, he was responsible for putting me in this predicament, and I was mad at him for it, but I never lost love for that man, still to this day. I would secretly go to his grave and talk to him. The only thing that was left of him was Luvleigh. She was the spitting image of both her parents, and I hated that she hated me. Juliet brainwashed all of the Carters into believing that I was responsible for X's death, but I had nothing to do with it. Never in a million years would I be the cause of my best friend's demise. If you think about it, who had the most to gain from his death?

I sat my boys down and told them what was really up. They knew the truth, and as much as I tried to talk them out of the hate they felt for the Carters, they couldn't stop hating them. After I was shot, my family was hit hard by all the financial problems that were created from X pulling his money from the company, as well as the artists. It left me bankrupt. I had to move my kids into a small two-bedroom apartment, where they were forced to survive off of Ramen noodles and Chef Boyardee until I could get back on my feet, figuratively speaking. I wasn't smart back then. I was spending money like that shit was going out of style. I saved nothing nor did I put anything up for a rainy day. I had ended up selling all of my cars. I even had to sell Romeo Jr.'s car, my boy's seventy-two-inch television, their game systems, and sneakers. You name it, I sold it, just to make ends meet. My kid's lives were ruined because of me, but they didn't see it that way. They refused to see any wrong in their father, instead, they chose to release their hate and anger on X's family.

Besides the big brawls, the beef never went any further than that. That's how I would have preferred to keep it, but something told me that Juliet would go the length to protect her secrets, and if someone had to get really hurt, then so be it.

"You can stop, sweetie," I told the girl, tapping her on top of her head. She was really trying her best to get me up, but it wasn't working.

"I'm sorry, big daddy. I tried my best," she said.

"I know. You've earned your money, love."

"Is there anything that turns you on? Maybe you can think about that and we can see if it works. How about if you watched me play with myself?" she suggested.

"Nah, it ain't gon' work. Your money is inside the drawer," I told her. She helped me pull my pants up before jumping off of the bed to collect her money. She got dressed and then came back on the bed.

"Call me if you need me to try again. Maybe I can wear a wig, different makeup, contacts. You let me know, alright, big daddy."

"Thanks, love," I said to her. She smiled and pecked me on the lips before climbing over me, leaving out of the bedroom door. I laid in the bed looking up at the ceiling. A tear rolled down my eye, but I swiped it away. This was my punishment for fucking another man's wife. Never being able to use my dick again.

There was a knock on the door. "Sir, are you good?" Rudy asked from the other side of the door.

"Yeah, I'm good, Ru, you can go home. I'll see you in the morning," I told him.

"Alright boss, see you tomorrow."

I heard his heavy ass feet walking away as I sat there, staring at the ceiling until I fell asleep.

BERNIECE

J woke up to someone knocking on the door. I looked over at Petey, who was sleeping through the banging. I twisted my lips up at him because the sight of him caused my stomach to turn. I haven't seen or heard from Dagger in weeks, and I had a feeling he was never coming back home. I had to put up with Petey because if Dagger wasn't coming back, I needed a new sponsor. I nudged him with my elbow hard as fuck. He jumped up quickly.

"What is it? Is it the baby?" he asked.

"No!"

"Ok, as long as my baby is ok in there," he said, laying back down and turning over. I rolled my eyes at his stupid ass really believing that he might have been the father of this baby. He was just being used for his money. I nudged him again.

"Get up, get dressed."

There was another knock on the door and I got up, grabbed my robe, and walked to the door. I looked through the peephole and it was a man in a suit. I opened it.

"Can I help you?" I asked.

"Yes, my name is Javier Consuela, and this is for you. It's your eviction notice. Mr. Masters put this house on the market two days ago and it was purchased by a lovely family who's looking to move in as soon as possible, so you have twenty-four hours to vacate the premises," he said, smiling and then walking off. Before getting into his car, he banged a sign into the front lawn that said sold.

I slammed the door and ran upstairs to get my cell phone. I called Dagger, although he hasn't been answering me. Surprisingly, he answered the phone.

"Got your eviction notice," a female voice answered the phone.

"Who the fuck is this, and why are you answering my man's phone?" I asked her.

"Your man? From the way you were sucking homeboy's dick the other night, I would have assumed he was your man."

"What? Who the fuck is this and where is Dagger?"

"This is Luvleigh and *my* fiancé, is right here. He don't want to talk to ya scandalous ass. He just wants you out, and when that baby is born, we will be up there to get a DNA test done. Oh, yeah, and one more thing. You've been evicted from that apartment my fiancé has been wasting his money paying for only for you to be shacking up in his house with yo' nigga. Ya shit has been placed on the curb for the garbage. It comes in two hours, so you better get to moving," Luvleigh said, hanging up on me. I was heated. I threw my phone into the wall and it shattered.

"You alright, B?" Petey asked. I wanted to go off on him, but I needed him now more than ever.

"No, I was evicted from my apartment, as well as this house. My things were placed out on the curb, do you think you can come over there with me to pick my things up."

"Of course. I'll do anything for you, B, you know that."

"Cool. I'm going to go put some clothes on," I told him as I walked up stairs and got dressed.

It didn't take me long, but I was pulling up to my apartment building, and just like Luvleigh said, all of my shit was outside. You could tell people had been rummaging through my shit. I pulled in front of it and directed Petey to pull up behind me so that we could start loading as much of it into our cars.

They were definitely going to pay for this shit.

LUVLEIGH

I rang Hunter's doorbell and then walked in. I didn't see my brother's car out there, so I knew he wasn't here because I wasn't going to walk into no fuck-a-thon.

"Bitch, where you at?" I called as I walked into the living room.

"I'm back here, hoe," she responded, and I followed her voice into her bathroom. She was sitting on the toilet with her hand between her legs.

"What the hell you doing?" I asked as she brought her hand from between her legs, revealing the pregnancy test. "Oh my god, are you pregnant, bitch?"

"We're about to find out in two minutes. I hope I am not."

"What you mean? You should be honored to be carrying my niece or nephew," I told her. She looked up at me with the 'bitch, bye' face.

"Girl, have you seen the size of your brother. I am not trying to be pushing out no fucking black Paul Bunyan. Big ass Iron Giant. Nah, not me, and your mother pushed out two of them motherfuckers. I don't know how she recovered after that."

"Bitch don't be talking about my brothers."

She sat the test down on the sink, wiped, and pulled her panties up. After she washed her hands, we left out the bathroom, leaving the test sitting on the sink.

"What's up with you, trick?" she asked, as we walked into her bedroom and she started to slip on some clothes.

"You might want to sit down for this," I told her, grabbing onto her arms and moving her to the bed, while she still had her pants around her ankles.

"Oh boy, what the fuck did you do? Do we have to bury a body?"

"No."

"Then what, because you scaring me."

"I'm getting married and I need you as a witness." She sat there for a second looking at me like I had three heads, then she burst out laughing. I stood there with my arms folded across my chest, tapping my foot, and waiting for her to stop laughing. Every time she would stop, she would start back up again. "Bitch is you done, or is you finished?"

"Alright, alright, I'm done."

"Like I said, I need you to be a witness."

"First of all, who the fuck you getting married to?" she asked me with a hint of laughter.

"Dagger," I answered. Her mouth dropped open and then she started to laugh again.

"Bitch, I know you fucking lying."

"I'm really not. He and I are getting married tomorrow, and I need a witness, and you're the only one I know that isn't judgmental. At least I thought."

"You damn right, I'm being judgmental. You barely know that man—"

"I do," I replied, cutting her off.

"You don't. He has a whole baby on the way—"

"So."

"Both of y'all families hate each other. I mean, like Capulets and Montague... hold the fuck up, you two tryna be Romeo and Juliet part three? Every Romeo and Juliet story ends tragically. Do you not remember what happens at the end of that story? They end tragically. The Shakespeare Romeo and Juliet story ended with the two of them dead, your mother and Dagger's father's little love affair story ended up with Romeo Sr. getting paralyzed from the waist down. There's too much bad blood between the two of your families. This love story is forbidden. Your father is probably turning over in his grave, Luvleigh."

I stood there looking at my best friend as a tear rolled down my face. "Really, Hunt?" I asked as I turned and walked away. I was almost at the door when I heard her calling after me.

"Luv, wait!" she called, but I kept on walking. I grabbed the doorknob. "Luvleigh, wait. I'm sorry," she replied, stopping me from opening the door.

"Sorry for what, Hunter? I know you, and I know you never say shit you don't mean. I get that this shit is forbidden as you say, but I want to be with Dagger, and he wants to be with me as well. And we are not going to allow this stupid ass feud between our families to keep us apart. Dagger and I know that this is all of a sudden, but we don't care. When have you known me to play by anyone's rules but my own? Never. Before my father died, he told me not to let anyone try and tell me who I am. The only person who truly knows who I am, is me. Play by my own rules, because it's a 50/50 chance that I'll lose playing by someone else's rules. Trust in your heart and that's what I'm doing. So, no, he's not turning over in his grave, he's rooting for me, and I thought you would be too."

"You're right, and I am here for it. I just want to make sure you know what you are about to do. I don't want to be a witness to my best friend's downfall, but if you are sure, then I'm here for you."

"Thank you!"

We hugged. "I guess his ass is getting what he always said he wanted," she said.

"What's that?"

"To be married to you. He been saying that shit since we were what? Thirteen?"

"Girl, twelve. Did you check your piss test?" I asked Hunter.

"I did, and I won't be pushing out a Godzilla. My pussy will stay intact. Won't he do it."

I laughed. "You are so stupid. You know you can't tell my brother, right? At least not before I tell them."

"I know. My loyalty is to you first. So when is this wedding and where, and what do I have to wear?"

"Well, it's tomorrow. We were supposed to go down to City Hall, but he said there was a change in the plan. I'll find out the location tomorrow. I'm going to stay here tonight if you don't mind."

"Not at all."

"And you can wear whatever, just make sure it's pretty."

"Ok, so that means you're taking me on a shopping trip, money bags?" she asked, looking at me with stern eyes that meant she was dead ass serious.

"Fine, since I'm paying, I'm picking the outfit out."

"Bitch, I don't give a shit. You have better taste then I do," she stated as she sat down on the couch and began to put her sneakers on. "Oh god, you know Ladi is going to be pissed."

"I don't care. Her ass been acting real strange lately."

"Seriously. I know good dick can make you go crazy, but damn. That bitch totally checked out the other night."

"Whatever, she'll find out when the rest of the family finds out. Come on, so we can hit the mall before people start getting out of work and crowding that shit up."

After spending the next two hours in the mall, we finally found the perfect dress for the both of us.

"Thank you, bestie," Hunter sang happily, as she intertwined her arm in mine and laid her head on my shoulder. She managed to get herself a Dolce and Gabbana dress that cost almost two grand. She lucky as fuck it was for my damn wedding, or else her ass would have gotten a fucking dress from Ten Spot. Sike, nah, I wouldn't do my girl like that, but her ass wouldn't have gotten no damn 2,000-dollar dress.

I managed to snag myself a beautifully studded Balmain gown. I wasn't sure what Dagger had planned, but he told me to get something nice to wear. This dress was perfect. It wasn't too dull, nor was it too flashy. I didn't want to buy any shoes because I had tons at home that would go perfectly with my dress.

"Yeah, yeah, yeah, whatever. Consider this your birthday gift as well," I told her.

"Girl, I know you just playing, so I ain't even gon' trip out on you right now," she said, placing a kiss on my cheek. "My bestie is getting married. I can't wait to see what married Luvleigh looks like."

"Uh, just like single Luvleigh, girl. Ain't nothing gon' change but my last name, address, and Facebook status, just to fuck with that bitch, Berniece."

"I can't wait until the two of you come to blows again so you can whoop her ass again, and the both of you can move the fuck on. You won, she lost."

"Her mouth is out of control. I just wanna make her swallow her fucking teeth."

She chuckled as we continued to walk through the parking lot to find my car. "So have y'all thought about you guys' financial aspect. He has dough, you have more dough, do you think it's going to be an inferiority thing between the two of you?"

"Not at all. Dagger isn't even like that. He's proud of where he is financially because he worked for it and earned it. He didn't inherit it like I did. Besides, if he ever needed anything, I would more than gladly give it to him. I been looking for an investment for all of my dough. I wouldn't mind investing in his car washes. You know, opening up a few more washes, bring in more money. He probably won't let me, but I'll convince him. I have my ways."

"Eeooow. My bitch a porn star now. What's the first thing y'all gon' buy as a couple? A house?"

"Me? Another fucking car!" I shouted once I laid eyes on my brand-new Porsche that looked like a fucking toddler had been let loose with a can of spray paint and scissors.

"Holy fucking shit!" Hunter cursed. Someone had spray painted the word 'homewrecker' on my shit in white, and then spray painted my windows every different color of the fucking rainbow, and all my tires were flat.

"This is some fucking bullshit. I'm fucking this bitch up, I swear."

"How do you know it was Berniece?"

I looked at Hunter like she was fucking dumb.

"Bitch, who the fuck else would spray paint *homewrecker* on my damn car?" I asked, shaking my head at her. The way she was taking up for the tramp was getting on my fucking nerves. I removed my phone and took a picture of my car, sending it to Dagger. The read message showed up telling me that he had seen it. My phone started ringing immediately.

"Hey, baby. Berniece did that shit?" he asked.

"Yeah. We were coming out from the mall and my car was like this."

"I'll get it fixed up. I'm coming to get you," he stated.

"No, I'm going to call Tink and have him come get us. I need to stop at my house, anyway. You can send someone to get my car though."

"Alright. I'll send someone from the shop. Where you going to stay tonight?"

"With Hunter, at her place."

"Nah, I have y'all a suite at the Ocean Place resorts in Sea Bright, later on a car is going to come pick you two up and bring you to the location, aight?"

"What's the location? Why won't you tell me anything?"

"Because I want my bride to be surprised. Give Hunter my number tell her to give me a call."

"Why?"

"Luvleigh, just do what the fuck I say, stop asking so many damn questions, girl."

I pulled the phone from my ear and looked at it, trying to figure out who he thought he was talking too.

"Nigga, you must've forgot who you're talking to. I'm not Berniece, I will smack yo' ass."

"And you will get smacked the fuck back. I know you're not

146

Berniece, but you will do as I say, you hear me? Tomorrow's going to be perfect."

"I believe it. Alright, I will see you tomorrow then, I guess."

"Alright, beautiful. I love you, Luvleigh," he said, making me smile.

"I love you too, Romeo," I replied, before hanging up the phone. I looked up at Hunter and she was just staring at me. "Why the fuck are you looking at me like that?" I asked her.

"I can't believe this is really going to happened." She smiled and then walked over to me as we walked back to the mall, waiting for Tink to come pick us up.

"THANKS, Tink. We're not going to be long. I just have to look for some shoes and then you can drop us off at Hunter's place."

"No problem, Luv," Tink agreed. I shut the door and ran into the house.

Hunter had already come in before me and ran her little fast ass to Star's room.

I immediately ran upstairs to my room to search for my Jimmy Choo Viola crystal stilettos that I had, but never worn. I paid 3,000 dollars for them things and never worn them. I made sure those were the first things I packed when I left school.

I searched up and down my closet and couldn't find them shits. "Where the fuck could they be?" I pondered. I left out my room and went to check my mother's room. I knocked on her door before I walked in. She wasn't here, so I just went into her huge ass closet and the lights turned on automatically due to the motion detector. My mom's closet was like a movie star's closet. She had shoes from the floor to ceiling, covering one entire wall. It had to be over two hundred pairs of damn shoes, and I thanked God they were color coordinated. It didn't take me long before I realized that they weren't here.

Down in the basement, I searched the storage area where my things were and that's where I found them, along with some of my other shit that I had no idea was missing. This bitch must've removed everything that she didn't buy or wasn't designer and threw them down here. I sifted through some of my things and made a pile of shit that I was bringing right back upstairs with me.

I stood up and was walking out the storage room when I noticed my dad's cherry wood chest with the gold trimmings. I haven't seen this in years. My dad kept all of his important things in there. It wasn't as shiny as it was when my dad was alive. It was dusty as hell and had been neglected. I was taking this trunk with me when I moved up out of here.

I kneeled down in front of it and brushed my hand across the top of it, swiping some of the dust off and then opening it. Tears started to form in my eyes as the faint smell of my daddy's cologne graced my nostrils.

"Oh, daddy. I miss you so much," I wept. "I wish I could have done more to help you. Help the police find the people who did this to you. I'm getting married, daddy. I know you probably wouldn't approve of it, but I know you wouldn't have stopped me. You always said to follow my heart and that's what I'm doing."

I reached into the trunk and began removing all the picture frames that contained family pictures with my dad. I did notice when I came back from school that there weren't any family pictures up anymore. Just pictures of Juliet.

I came across the picture of my daddy and I at my fifth birthday party. I was dressed up as a princess, and my daddy was dressed up like a king. Juliet refused to participate, but that didn't stop me from having one of the best birthdays ever. I placed the picture down and then picked up what looked like my mother's wedding rings, just thrown into the trunk. They were sitting on top of their wedding photo. I picked up the picture and looked at it as I did many times before. I dreamt of being as beautiful as Juliet was in this picture. I placed it down on the floor next to me and noticed something gold tucked in the corner. After fishing it I out, I realized it was my dad's gold Rolex. I looked at it and started having flashbacks to the night my father was shot.

I remember my dad having this watch on when he got out of the car to go inside the mart, but I don't remember him having it on when I was doing CPR on him. I thought the robbers took it. Maybe I was mistaken. It could have just rolled up his arm. It was still ticking. It was such a beautiful watch for it to just sit inside of a trunk. I put it on my arm.

As I continued to maneuver things around, I found a velvet pink box with my name on it. I had never seen it before. The box was really beautiful. I unlatched it and opened up the top. There was glitter tissue paper as soon as I opened it. I moved it away and my eyes popped open. It was the pink and chrome Desert Eagle my dad had promised me. My name was engraved on it. It was so beautiful.

"Aww, you did get it for me. Thank you, daddy." I picked it up from the box and examined it. Under the gun was a note. I opened the folded piece of paper.

My dearest baby girl, Luvleigh. Although it's my birthday, you are my greatest accomplishment. Being able to provide you with all the things you want, brings me the most joy. I love you more than life itself. Stay strong, stay brave, follow your heart, and remember that I'm always here for you. Always and Forever.

Love, Daddy

By the time I was done reading the letter, my face was flooded with tears. He was going to give this to me on his birthday, but he didn't have the chance because he was killed. I folded the paper back up and placed it where I got it from, and then tucked the gun back in its position before shutting the top.

After I placed everything back inside of the trunk, I shut it and then went to go grab the rest of my things.

Once I got into my bedroom, I packed some clothes inside of my LV duffle bag. I looked at the watch once again, and then I placed it inside my bag along with the gun.

I had everything packed and went to go find Hunter. She was

coming up from the basement at the same time I was coming down the stairs. She was all sweaty and shit.

"You are fucking terrible. Let's go girl."

"Don't judge me, bitch. I'm addicted to the dick," she replied, as we left out the house.

LIKE DAGGER PROMISED, there was a car sitting outside Hunter's place waiting for us. After she ran into the house and packed a few things, we were on our way to the hotel.

The hotel was freaking beautiful. It was right off of the beach. The suite overlooked the ocean. The hotel staff spent the last few hours pampering Hunter and I with a massage, manicure and pedicures, facials, you name it. Then we dined on top of the line filet mignon and champagne. Everything was being charged to Dagger's card. I had to be sure to thank him.

By the time we got back to our suite, we were so relaxed that the both called it a night and went straight to our rooms. After getting out of the shower, I dressed in one of Dagger's t-shirts I kept after one of our sexual rendezvous. It still smelled like him.

I tried calling Dagger, but I got no answer. This was probably the first night in a long time going to bed without seeing him, which made it hard for me to fall asleep. I opened up the patio doors so that I could listen to the ocean waves that crashed just below my patio. I laid there, staring at my wedding dress and thinking about my future with Dagger. All the good and the bad things that were going to come but still didn't make me second guess what I was about to do. I was following my heart.

I don't know when, but I ended up falling asleep. I was soon awakened by something touching my lips. I jumped up out my sleep but was forced back down onto the bed. I looked behind me and instantly relaxed once I laid eyes on his handsome face.

"You scared me," I told him, nuzzling his chest.

"I'm sorry, I just wanted to see you. You know, we've been seeing each other every night for the past twenty-one days. I became so accustomed to seeing you every day, it's a little hard to go to sleep without seeing my baby girl."

"Isn't that something. I was feeling the same way, but I started to think about you, and us, and our future, and it helped me fall asleep."

"I'm a man, baby, I need the real thing."

"It's bad luck for the groom to see the bride before the wedding."

"I don't give a shit about all of that. I do what I want. Didn't I tell you I'm savage, baby."

"Shut up. You ain't no fucking savage. You's a damn teddy bear."

"Don't fucking play with me," he said, playfully smacking my cheek. I placed my small fist on the middle of his head.

"Don't get knocked out the night before your wedding, homie," I joked. We both shared a laugh and then he stood up before walking over to the dresser and grabbed something.

"I have something for you," he said as he walked back over and climbed into the bed behind me.

"What is it?" I asked.

"Open it."

I sat up and opened the royal blue velvet box, displaying a big, beautiful diamond ring. It glistened under the moonlight that illuminated the room.

"I never got you one, so I figured I would get you one before we get married. To make it official," he spoke in an intimate tone. I looked over at him and then back at the ring.

"This is really beautiful. Did you pick it out?" I asked.

"With 4Dz' help."

He took the box from my hand and then removed the ring. "Give me your hand." I gave him my left hand. "Tomorrow will be the first day of the rest of our life. You ready for that?"

"As long you're by my side, I'm ready for anything," I responded lovingly. I gently grabbed his perfect face and kissed his soft, thick lips. "I can't wait until tomorrow so I can kiss you whenever I want."

"It's already tomorrow," he said, giving a head nod toward the clock that read 1:10 a.m. I smiled and turned back to him. I kissed him again, locking my lips onto his as our tongues danced in each other's mouths.

I climbed onto his lap, never breaking our kiss. Reaching into his pants, I grabbed his dick, and it grew inside of my hand. I pulled it out and stroked his dick up and down. Quickly breaking our kiss, I released a little spit from my mouth, allowing it to drip down onto the tip of his dick. I used my spit to get his dick wet, which made it easier for me to slowly slide down on it. My head dropped back in pleasure once I felt him opening me up as I slowly moved up and down.

Dagger grabbed on to the back of my neck, bringing it to his mouth, and he sucked on my neck, arousing my body even more than it already was. I could feel myself getting wetter with every pounce.

"Shit, Luvleigh, baby. You're really learning to fuck this dick up, girl," he muttered through moans.

"I was taught by the best, baby."

"That's right. Take all this dick because it's yours. Always and forever."

Hearing him say "always and forever", which was the same thing my daddy always said, erased any and every doubt I ever had about my love for Dagger.

My moans filled the room the same way that my tears filled my eyes. I was so in love with this man, and I couldn't wait to be his wife.

"I'm about to nut, baby," he warned.

"Ok."

"In or out?" he asked me like he always did. Usually, I would say out, but at this moment, I wanted all of him. Every ounce, every inch, every drop.

"In," I answered. He pulled back and his eyes burned into mine.

"You sure?" he asked. I nodded my head. With that, he laid me on my back and stroked every inch of himself in and out of me, until he was releasing every drop inside of me.

He laid on top of me panting. I wrapped my arms around his neck as he rolled over, rolling me on top of him. I laid there, snuggled into his armpit.

"I love you, Dagger."

"I love you too, Luvleigh," he replied, kissing me on my forehead. I closed my eyes and drifted off to sleep.

~

I woke up to Hunter kicking in my room door. I jumped up, looking around for Dagger.

"Looking for husband-to-be?" she asked. "He left like an hour ago."

I pulled the sheet up, covering my titties after realizing that I was still naked. Hunter came over with a bowl in her hand and jumped onto the bed. She dug into the bowl and started raining red rose petals all over me.

"It's your wedding day, Mrs. Masters."

"I know. I can't believe it," I said.

"I can. I heard all the love in here last night, and I'm convinced," she said as she continued to jump. "That must've been some good ass dick the way yo' ass was in here moaning," she joked, and then started to mimic the way I was moaning.

"Oh my god, stop it," I told her as I placed the cover over my head, embarrassed.

She dropped down on top of me in a straddle position and began grinding on me. "O' Romeo, O' Romeo, wherefore art thou Romeo?" she mocked, causing me to laugh.

"Oh my God, get the fuck off of me you damn looney tune." I pushed her off of me and then climbed out of the bed, wrapping a sheet around my naked body. "I'm going to shower, so I can meet my baby."

"Yup, I can't wait to meet y'all baby, too." I turned and looked at her. She stood up from the bed. "These walls are thin, sis. I heard you tell him to nut in you," she stated, walking past me while smacking me on the ass.

I shook my head, laughed, and then walked into my bathroom to take a shower.

DAGGER

$\mathcal{A}$fter I left Luvleigh this morning, I drove back to the place where the wedding was going to happen at. The hotel where Luv was staying, was only ten minutes away from where the venue was. I left 4Dz in charge of making sure everything would be perfect. I told her to tap into her girl side, and she wasn't feeling that. I had to put her little ass in a headlock real quick to remind her who the real nigga was around here.

The venue where the wedding was going to be taking place, was called Windows on The Water, and I paid a lot of money for this place to accommodate us with such short notice. They were fine with it because it was just us four and the officiant.

"Everything set for tonight?" I asked 4Dz, walking into the room. She had a blunt in her hand with her legs kicked up, watching television.

"You know this," she replied, mimicking Smoky from the movie *Friday.*

"Cool. I appreciate you, 4Dz."

"I know. Come sit next to me," she ordered, patting the space beside her. I walked over and sat down next to her. She passed me the blunt. "How's Luvleigh? Is she serious about this marriage?"

"Yeah. I believe she is. She's here, right?"

"Yeah, she is…. Ok then. Here's to you," she said, picking up her drink and raising it in the air. "Congratulations, nigga."

I sat back with her watching television. The vibration of my phone caught my attention. It was Berniece. I threw the phone back down, ignoring her ass. She wasn't about to ruin my day. She called about four more times before her ass gave up.

"Fuck was that?" 4Dz asked.

"Berniece's ass."

"What you gon' do about her?"

"I don't fucking know," I answered with a shrug of my shoulders.

"How far along is she?"

"Five months… I think. She could be four. I really don't give a fuck."

She nodded her head in acceptance. We sat back, getting high and watching TV until I stood up to walk into my room. I shut the door and fell out on the bed. Before falling asleep, I set my alarm to wake me up at six, just in case I didn't wake up before then.

BERNIECE

$\mathcal{J}$ sat inside of my bubble bath, sipping on some red wine. According to my doctor, it was ok if I had a glass of wine at night. I had been trying to call Dagger, but he was ignoring my ass and sending me to voicemail. I was pissed the fuck off. First, he left me pregnant and homeless, and then he allowed that bitch, Luvleigh, to talk to me all crazy and shit, talking about he's her fiancé. I knew her ass was lying and just trying to make me jealous, but that wasn't going to happen. I had his baby. He was going to be stuck with me for the rest of his fucking life. I picked my phone up from the side of the bathtub and snapped a picture of my naked body in the bathtub before sending it to Dagger

I started to scroll through Facebook when I came across Hunter's post.

When a man finds something good, he drops three carats on it and changes that last name. #becausemybestfriendfina #gobestfriend #trueLuv

Under that post was a picture of a big ass diamond ring sitting inside of a velvet box with the caption: *#Daaaaggggggg*

"What the fuck!" I shouted, throwing my phone into the wall; this time it didn't break. I grabbed my towel and got out of the bath, covering my body. I read between the lines. Those posts were about Luvleigh and Dagger.

"Everything alright?" Petey asked, coming into the bathroom.

"Yeah," I lied. He bent down to pick up my phone.

"You sure?" he asked, rubbing my belly. I smacked his hand away, trotting into the bedroom. I started to get dressed. "Where are you going?" Petey asked. He was really starting to annoy the fuck out of me.

"Out. I have to go do something."

"Ok, well, be safe. I'll have some food ready for you when you get back."

I sucked my teeth and rolled my eyes. "Oh my God, Petey. Will you grow some fucking balls? You act so damn soft sometimes. You gon' have a plate on the table waiting on me? What kind of bitch shit is that?" I asked him. He just stood there looking at me with this dumb facial expression before turning to walk out of the room. I suddenly felt bad. I had to remember that this was the only place I had to go as of now.

"Hey," I called, stopping him by grabbing on to his arm. He turned around slowly. "I'm sorry. I'm just a little hormonal with the baby and all. It's all your fault. You knocked me up," I coaxed him. He started to smile. "How about when I come back, I show you how sorry I am."

"I'm down for it," he affirmed and then kissed me on the lips.

I continued to get dressed before I grabbed my keys to leave out of the house.

I met Petey at a party like two years ago. He was a music producer for BRIKZ. I accompanied Petey to an album release party, which was where I met Dagger. Dagger knew I was there with Petey, and he ain't give a shit. He saw what he wanted, and he took that shit. That's what I liked in a nigga. I knew I had caught a big fish when it came to Dagger, so I did everything I needed to do to make sure I kept him. I gave him the best head and gave him the best pussy, but he still ain't wife my ass. Instead, he started messing with that chick Maxine. I doubt if she fucked like me. Her or that bitch, Luvleigh. I don't see what he saw in her that he didn't see in me. You know what, fuck him and fuck her. I had something for them both.

It was five minutes to seven. The carwash should have been closing in any minute, but Dagger usually stayed around a few minutes after. Until I was sure he was gone, I drove around, collecting everything I was going to need. By the time I got everything, I was back at the carwash at five after seven and it was closed. I guess Dagger didn't want to stick around since he had his little fiancée waiting on him.

"Good," I said to myself as I got out the car and walked around to my trunk. I grabbed the red gasoline canister and the box of matches. Once I arrived at the building, I began to douse it with gasoline while singing, "Dame mas gasolina. Dame mas gasolina."

I got halfway around the building before I had to run back to the car and grab the second canister for the second half of the building.

"Goodbye, carwash," I said, sitting the canister down. I removed the matches from my pocket and flicked one on. I gave the carwash one last look before I threw the match as the building suddenly went up in flames.

Dagger

"It's go time, nigga," 4Dz informed me as she adjusted my attire. I was dressed in a long-sleeved button up polo shirt, that was cuffed to my elbows, and a gray Armani suit vest with the matching pants. It was on a beach, so I was going to be barefoot.

The ceremony was going to take place on the beachfront, under an arch that was decorated in white sheer drapes with red roses and lights. White candles inside of lanterns will light up the walkway, which was sprinkled with white and red rose petals, that also lead down a path where we're to stand and get married. Everything was perfect. I just needed her to get her ass down here so that I could wife her little ass already.

I stood under the arch waiting. I knew that women took long getting ready, but damn. I checked my rollie and realized another five minutes had gone by. I was just about to send 4Dz to go check on her when she came walking down the walkway with Hunter following behind. She had the biggest, brightest smile on her face. I could see it from all the way down here. The dress she wore had clung to her body perfectly. She wore her hair up and into a bun with close to no makeup. The only makeup I could see was lipstick, and that's all she needed. That's how queens got married.

She was a few inches from me when I grabbed her hand and yanked her into my arms. I couldn't wait to touch her. The officiant cleared his throat to grab our attention.

"My bad," I said, releasing her.

"It's beautiful," she spoke with a smile.

"Are we ready to get started?" the officiant asked. We both gave a head nod and grabbed each other's hands.

"Let's make this short and sweet," I told him.

As he started to speak, our eyes burned into each other, and they stayed that way throughout the entire ceremony. It was like no one else was on that beach but us. I felt like I was in a fucking Disney movie, and the two of us were being carried away by the stars. She was really bringing out the bitch in me and I was ok with that. I was stirred from my little fantasy by the ringing of my phone.

"Shit, my bad," I said, reaching into my pocket and removing my phone before throwing it to 4Dz. She shut it down and placed it inside her pocket.

The officiant continued, and I went back to staring into the eyes of my love, getting lost in her smile.

"Today, we have come together to witness the joining of these two lives. For them, out of the routine of ordinary life, the extraordinary has happened. They met each other, fell in love, and are finalizing it with their wedding. A good marriage must be created. It is never being too old to hold hands. It's remembering to say I love you every day, and it is not just marrying the right person, it's being the right partner. Should there be anyone who has cause why this couple should not be united in marriage, speak now."

We looked around to the only two people who were present, and they both shook their heads no.

"Great, let us continue. Romeo, repeat after me."

"I, Romeo, take you, Luvleigh, to be my wife, my partner in life, and my one true love. I will cherish our friendship and love you today, tomorrow, always and forever," I vowed.

"Now, Luvleigh, repeat after me."

"I, Luvleigh, take you Romeo, to be my husband, my partner in life and my one true love. I will cherish our friendship and love you today, tomorrow, always and forever," she vowed.

"Beautiful. Romeo, do you take Luvleigh to be your wife?"

"I do," I answered strong and confidently, without hesitation.

"Do you promise to love, honor, cherish, and protect her, forsaking all others and holding only unto her?"

"I do."

"Luvleigh, do you take Romeo to be your husband?"

"I do, with all of my heart," she answered, making me smile.

"Do you promise to love, honor, cherish, and protect him, forsaking all others and holding only unto him?"

"I do."

"The rings please," he asked. 4Dz passed me the band while Hunter passed Luvleigh the hers. "Romeo, repeat after me. This ring is my sacred gift, with my promise that I will always love you, cherish you, and honor you all the days of my life. And with this ring, I thee wed."

I repeated after him, placing the band on Luvleigh's finger. As I was doing that I could hear the vibration of my phone, which was in 4Dz' pocket. I tried my best to ignore it, but I was curious to know who the fuck was blowing my damn phone up. If it was Berniece, I was going to smack the shit out her ass.

"Luvleigh, repeat after me as you place the ring upon Romeo's finger."

She did as she was told, placing the band on my finger.

"By the power vested in me, I now pronounce you, husband and wife. You may kiss your bride."

The moment he said I could kiss my bride, I tongued her down for about a good minute.

"We're married," she said.

"We sure are, Mrs. Luvleigh Masters. You ready to go tell the world?" I asked her. She shook her head no. "Well you better get ready."

4Dz and Hunter walked up to us, congratulating us. I could still hear my phone vibrating in her pocket.

"Who the fuck is that?" I asked. She removed it from her pocket and showed me that it was my pops. I took the phone and answered it. "Pops, what's going on?" I asked.

"The carwash is on fire," he informed me.

"What?" I asked for clarification, although I didn't really need any. I heard him perfectly. "I'm on my way." I hung up the phone and looked over at Luvleigh.

"What's going on?" she asked.

"My carwash is on fire."

A WEEK LATER

LADI

I sat on my bed with my results in my hand. I had just come to the doctor and I was beyond pissed. With my phone to my ear, I paced back and forth, waiting on Tr8z to answer the phone, and I wasn't going to stop until he did. I didn't give a fuck if he got mad.

"Tr8z, answer the fucking phone!" I shouted as I got his voicemail before hanging up and redialing his number. My phone beeped, alerting me that another call coming in. Thinking it was Tr8z calling me back, I clicked over without really looking. "What the fuck Tr8—"

"Tr8z?" Luvleigh asked. I removed the phone from my ear and looked at the screen before placing it back to my ear. "Why are you talking to Tr8z?" she asked, causing me to become annoyed. More annoyed than I already was.

"Luvleigh, I don't have time for this right now. I'll call you back," I told her, hanging the phone up on her. I knew I wasn't going to hear the end of that, but honestly, I really wasn't in the mood to hear about Luvleigh and her perfect little life.

Almost my entire life I lived in Luvleigh's shadow. I was older than she was, but she was the princess of the family. I didn't have it as good as she did. Not saying that I had a shitty life or anything because I didn't. I just wasn't as privileged as Luvleigh.

My mother couldn't hold a job to save her damn life. She had a bad attitude, and she was a damn drunk. My mother had a serious problem with authority which was why she was always getting fired.

We almost lost the house until my aunt Juliet looked out for us, which wasn't a surprise. My mom and aunt were close, almost best friends. Since I could remember, Juliet had always looked out for us. She helped my mother start her own wig business, which was how we were able to maintain our living. My father, on the other hand, wasn't really shit but a damn tweaker. I'm surprised he and my mother were still together, but I'm happy that they are.

My dad worked in sanitation for years. He was making close to 50,000 dollars a year until he went into work one day high and out of his damn mind, crashing the damn garbage truck into McDonalds. He cashed out his 401k, which was supposed to help out with the rent and bills, but his ass got high with that money.

"Fuck this," I said, putting my phone into my purse and walking out of my bedroom door. As I walked down the stairs, my father was coming up with a brown paper bag to his nose. I already knew he had a rag with paint thinner on it that was inside of the bag. He did that shit on the regular. I rolled my eyes, shook my head, and continued on my way.

I jumped into my red Infiniti Q50 and pulled off. Since this nigga wanted to ignore my phone calls, let's see how he ignored me when I pulled up on his ass.

It took me about thirty minutes to get here, and I spotted his Maserati parked in front of the studio. I pulled up behind it and jumped out. The security at the front desk knew who I was, shit, I let him hit a few times so I could meet some of the artist that recorded here. If my aunt found out that I was harassing her artists, she would curse my ass the fuck out.

"Hey Nick," I flirted.

"What's up, Ladi?" he asked.

"Shit, I need a favor."

"Oh yeah, what you gon' do for me?"

"Nothing right now, but you can consider it as an IOU."

"Alright. What you need?" he asked.

"I need to see Tr8z. He left his watch in my car the other day, I wanted to give it back to him," I lied, taking out one of my watches.

"Studio three."

I winked my eye at him and then turned to leave. I could feel him eyeing my ass which was all good. It ain't like he never seen it before. Shit, his face was in it a few times too.

I knew this building like the back of my hand, I just hoped my aunt wasn't in the building. She usually spent majority of her time inside of her office. She rarely came out unless it was to crack the whip on some of these artists that were slacking.

I turned the corner and then jumped back behind the wall. Out of all the days, her ass was here. Damnit. I peeked around the corner and she was looking down at some papers in her hand. Cream was running up behind her and wrapping his arms around her waist, kissing her on the neck. My mouth dropped open. I continued to peek at them until I saw her head turn toward my way, and I hid behind the wall again. Peeking back out, I knew she hadn't seen me because she grabbed the back of his neck and shoved her tongue down his throat. This was some shit. My aunt was half his age. How could they be fucking? She pushed him back into a wall as they continued to kiss. He broke the kiss and opened the door he was leaning against. He smiled, and Juliet walked in before him. He looked down both ends of the hallway and he spotted me, giving me that sexy ass panty-dropping smile before he walked into the room after my aunt, shutting the door behind him. Once the door shut, I stepped out from behind the wall. I couldn't believe my aunt was fucking her son's best friend. I wondered how she would feel if she knew I fucked him too.

"I know that's right, Aunty," I cheered her on.

If Cream was here, that meant the twins were here too, so I really had to be cool because Star's ass would pick me up by the neck and toss me out on my ass. He knew I was a gold-digging hoe, and there was only one reason why I was here. To be a hoe.

I finally made it to studio three, and I opened the door and walked in. Tr8z was sitting in there with a few of his niggas and a few bitches. One for all of them.

The door opening caught his attention. He looked over at me and I put on my attitude quick. I guess the bitch sitting in his lap was the reason why he was ignoring me. If you asked me, I looked two times better than her ass. I had beautiful milk chocolate skin, thick lips, bright round eyes. I was a living, breathing Bratz doll. I was fly as fuck, but of course all eyes stayed on Luvleigh.

"Can I talk to you?" I asked him.

"No," he responded.

"Fuck you mean no? I need to talk to ya ass so either get the fuck up and come out here and talk to me, or I will spill your business in front of everyone."

He rolled his eyes before standing up and walking over to me, pushing me out the door.

"What the fuck you want, Ladi?"

"Your phone broke or something?" I asked him. I noticed his jaws tightened. I figured I'd better get the fuck on with it. I removed the paper from my purse and handed it to him.

"Fuck is this?" he asked. "You pregnant?"

"I wish I was, but sorry, I didn't get that lucky. Keep reading."

"Ladi, even if I was to keep reading, I don't know what the fuck I'm reading."

I reached over the paper and pointed on the paper where it said, reactive to HSV-1.

"Fuck is that?"

"That means, yo' ass gave me fucking herpes," I told him, slapping the paper out his hand.

"Ok and?" he asked, causing me to gasp. "I knew I had it, just get the treatment or some shit," he had the nerve to say. I looked at him like he was stupid. The anger built up inside me and I knocked that nigga straight in the face. He grabbed on to the side of his face and before I could blink, he had my ass hemmed up on the wall, choking the shit out of me. My feet were dangling in the air. "You ever put your fucking hands on me again, I will fucking end your damn life, you hear me?" he asked. I nodded my head up and down and he let me go as I fell to the ground, gasping for air. "I knew I had that shit, but I don't give fuck. It ain't bothering me. If you care so much about your health, then you should have asked me to put a fucking condom on. Now get the fuck out of my damn face with all that bullshit, Ladi, and don't call my fucking phone again. Oh yeah, for your information, your cousin's pussy taste way better than yours," he said, walking back into the studio.

I stayed on the floor until I was able to catch my breath and pulled myself up. As I walked back toward the entrance of the building, tears fell from my eyes. I couldn't believe that he would just blatantly give me herpes. *Who does shit like that?* I asked myself. I wiped the tears from my eyes as I walked out into the summer night. The warm breeze hit my face, and it was like I could hear the petty gods whispering down upon me.

I walked over to the trunk of my car and popped it open. I removed the half-empty can of white spray paint and walked over to his Maserati. I prayed that I had enough spray paint as I started to create my masterpiece, seeing as though I had already used majority of it to spray paint 'Homewrecker' on Luvleigh's car. I know it was wrong, but she was wrong for getting in between Dagger and Berniece's relationship. By the time I was done, he had 'I HAVE HERPES' sprayed around the body of his car.

Juliet

"So what do you have for me?" I asked Cream as I straightened my skirt and searched the floor of the empty studio for my diamond earring that had come out from our quick fuck.

"You sure you want to know?" he asked. I looked up at him, giving him a look that answered his question.

"I wouldn't have asked you if I didn't want to know," I responded.

"Baby, I think Luvleigh and Dagger are married," he confessed.

"What? You're lying. She would never."

"Why would I lie about some shit like that? You ain't think she would be fucking him either, but she clearly was. I'm sorry, but your daughter doesn't give a fuck about the fam no more. She's a Master no—"

Before he could get the rest out, I slapped the spit out his mouth. He didn't do anything wrong, his words had just pissed me off. He was just telling me what I didn't want to hear. Telling me the truth. My daughter had deceived me. She'd deceived the family. He was right, she was a Masters.

"I'm sorry," I apologized to him, massaging the cheek that I smacked.

"It's cool. Just let me know what you want me to do."

I looked up at him. "Meet me at the house in an hour. There is something you can do. No one fucks us over. Oh, and don't tell my sons what you've discovered, I need to make sure she has truly turned against us before we tell anyone."

LUVLEIGH

onight was the Billboard music awards. G.O.A.T's newest artist, Nardi, won the Break Out Star of the year. That was the only one we brought home, but it was better than nothing. That's exactly what BRIKZ won. Not a damn thing. I would have texted Dagger to rub our win in his face, but it wasn't the time. He was still in a pissy mood about his carwash.

After he got the call about it being on fire, the four of us rushed straight home. It took about an hour to get there, but when we did, they had already managed to put the fire out. Dagger's place was destroyed. The fire department was still investigating, but so far, they had nothing and nobody.

I tried to talk him into coming tonight, thinking maybe it would help him take his mind off of it, but he refused. He was really depressed.

I've been out looking for our new place to live. I found a few that I liked, but I didn't feel comfortable choosing one without his input. He was going to be living there as well, so I wanted to make sure he liked it too.

We still hadn't told anyone, but I felt like Juliet knew something was up. She barely wanted to invite me tonight. She had Sun ask me to come. I wasn't sure what her problem was, but I didn't care. She would find out for sure, sooner or later. I just wanted to make sure that I had a place to go once I told her.

Ladi's ass also wasn't speaking to Hunter or me for some reason, but she was here tonight. She looked cute in hot pink shorts that hugged her booty with the matching suit jacket, which had a plunging neckline. I had on a royal purple skin tight dress that stopped mid-thigh. My hair was bone-straight, and my makeup was done beautifully. My mother bought this dress for me. I figured that if I wore it, it would make her a little happy, but nope. She still had a little 'tude. I took both of my rings off and just wore some costume jewelry.

I was happy the awards were in New York City this year, which meant I could take my ass straight home. Maybe sneak off to see my husband who I was dying without.

We had just pulled up to the after party and it was wild. We were shown to our seats, which were right across from the Masters. They weren't even paying attention to us sitting here, but my brothers were visibly bothered.

4Dz and I made eye contact before she gave a head nod in the direction in front of us. I looked to see what she as hinting at, and there my baby was. Walking in looking so freaking sexy, dressed in all white. He had on a pair of Balmain jeans and a white three-quarter sleeve shirt. He also had on his gold Jesus piece with some Balmain beige colored, medallion suede ankle boots. He had finally decided to cut his hair, and his waves were in rotation, and his beard was still nice and thick how I liked it.

I know that I said him coming here would have been a good thing for him to get his mind off of his car wash, but this shit was not going to be good for me. Having to sit here and look at him, without being able to touch him was killing me. I wanted to cry.

"Luvleigh, you looking over there kind of hard, you sure you don't want to go sit over there?" Juliet asked. I tore my eyes away from Dagger for a second and looked over at her.

"Wh—what?" I stuttered. "I'm not looking over there," I lied. She gave me the 'yeah ok' look before turning back to what she was doing.

"Here, have a drink," she said, handing me a glass of champagne. I took it from her and began sipping as I tried to look at other things rather than eyeballing my secret husband.

I watched the dance floor, trying to keep myself occupied. Hunter and I danced in our seats to Walking Trophy. My eyes involuntarily looked over to see Berniece walking toward Dagger. My blood was boiling, and Hunter knew it because she looked over at me before pushing my champagne glass up to my mouth for me to take a sip of my drink. I could feel the steam coming out my ears, my nose, mouth, ass, anything with a hole, steam was coming out of it.

I knew my reaction would not only give me away, but it would turn this motherfucker out. My brothers were looking for a reason to pounce, and I didn't want to give it to them. I sat the drink down because I started feeling a little woozy.

I looked back over to the Masters' section and found Berniece staring at me as she spoke to Dagger. She then had the nerve to sit down on his lap and I stood up abruptly. Everyone looked at me, and that's when Hunter stood up with me.

"Y'all already know it's time to hit the fucking dance floor, right?" she said, grabbing my hand. She pulled Ladi to her feet and the three of us left the area.

We walked down to the dance floor and the DJ done fucked up. Saweetie's song *Icy Girl* came on and we started to cut up on the floor. We danced as we rapped along to the song. I felt someone grab my waist and I turned around and it was some dude. I immediately pushed him off of me. He stood there trying to ask me why I didn't want to dance with him, but Hunter shut that shit down real quick, moving me out the way before we started to dance again. Ladi was off dancing with someone, leaving Hunter and I to dance with each other.

We were dancing to *She Bad* by Cardi B when I felt someone grab my wrist, and I went to snatch away, but this person had a grip on my shit. I looked to see who it was, and it was Dagger. He yanked my arm, pulling me closer to him.

"Go sit ya ass down with that tight ass dress on," he told me.

"Why was she sitting on your lap?"

"Because that bitch is stupid, you left before I made her ass get up. Now go sit the fuck down before you start some shit up in here."

I gave him a look and then rolled my eyes. Dagger ambled away. I grabbed Hunter's arm.

"Baby got put in the corner," I spoke into her ear.

"Ah damn." She laughed. "Alright, I'm going to stay down here with Ladi. Send your brother down here to dance with me."

I told her 'ok' before I strolled back over toward the area. As I was walking, someone purposely bumped into me hard, getting my attention. I looked up as I massaged my sore arm. Of course, it was Berniece. I was ready to jump on that bitch like a fucking Spider monkey, but then I looked down at her belly, and was able to contain myself. I had to remember that that was Dagger's baby inside of her. I rolled my eyes and turned back to go to my section where my mother, aunt, and brothers were sitting.

"Why didn't you knock her out?" Sun asked.

"She's pregnant. Star, Hunter said to bring your ass down to the dance floor."

He picked up his personal bottle of Remy and took it to the face before standing up and going to find Hunter.

I sat down on the couch. My mother picked up the bottle of Champagne she had next to her and reached over to pour me a drink.

"Thanks," I said, taking a sip of it.

"You never cared about her being pregnant before," Juliet added. I handed the glass over for her to pour me another drink.

"I guess I just don't have the time for that bitch anymore. I'll wait until she drops that baby, so she won't have any excuses."

I sipped on that last glass of champagne my mother poured me as I watched the room. The shit was really hitting hard. Normally, I could drink an entire bottle to myself. I guess I was becoming a lightweight.

"Hell-lo, Animal Kingdom," I heard my aunt Tammy say. I looked to see what had gotten her attention and I fell out laughing. This man was in the club in a floor length fur coat with no shirt under, and his chest oiled down. Mind you, it was summertime. It wasn't really that funny, but it was because I was drunk.

"Aunt Tammy, really? That's what you like?" I asked. "He looks like he stumbled in here by accident, looking for the Playa's Ball."

"Niece, that's real mink. I can see that from over here. It's a 50/50 chance he got gwap. He Tarzan, me Tammy. Watch me work niece," she said, fixing her appearance and then strutting off into the direction of her jungle king.

My mother and I sat there quietly, not really saying anything to each other. Every now and then I would catch her and Romeo give each other dirty looks. They were so fucking childish.

I sat up with my elbows in my knees and my head in the palms of my hands. I was dizzy and I was sweating profusely. I picked up one of the coasters and started fanning myself with it. I wasn't sure where Dagger went, but he hadn't come back to their section. I assumed he and 4Dz left or were at the bar.

"Why don't you step outside and get some air, Luvleigh," Juliet suggested. I agreed with her and then stood up. "Go to the back, there's probably still a lot of people out front," she added. I nodded my head and slowly made my way to the exit, following the exit signs to the back door. It started to feel like the walls were closing in on me, and I found it hard to breathe.

I walked as fast as I could until I was pushing the back door open and the air hit my face. I still felt tingly and my vision was blurred. There were milk crates by the dumpster, and I walked over and sat down.

As I sat, my body started to sway back and forth, and I felt like I was about to fall at any minute. Sitting seemed to be making it worse, so I tried standing up, but my knees became weak and I fell to the ground.

"Help!" I shouted out loud for someone to hear me, but it only came out as mere whisper. I felt someone wrap their arms around me and pick me up off the ground. I looked behind me, but I couldn't see anyone. "Dagger is that you?" I asked, but whoever it was didn't answer me.

I was being carried further and further away from the back door of the club. I was then thrown into the back of a van. Whoever it was,

was wearing a mask and climbed into the back of the van with me. My vision was blurred, but as the van's doors were closed, I could have sworn I seen my mother standing in the alleyway near the club's back exit.

"Who are you?" I asked the person. They didn't say anything, but I felt this person tugging at my dress and my underwear. I tried fighting back but I was too weak. My arms flailed around like noodles. "Don't touch me!" I shouted.

"Shut the fuck up!" A punch was delivered to my mouth. I could feel my tooth crack and my mouth fill up with blood. I spit it out onto the floor of the van.

"Why are you doing this?"

"Didn't I say shut the fuck up?"

Another blow was delivered to my already fucked up mouth. I rolled over into a fetal position with my hands covering my face. I was being rolled over onto my back and my hands were tied together as a piece of fabric was placed over my eyes. My legs were forcefully yanked apart. I tried to scream and fight, but I was too weak. I tried to kick, but it was prevented because he was between my legs, keeping them apart.

I gave up fighting after becoming exhausted, and I just laid there while whoever this was, violated my body. As he repeatedly entered me, it felt like I was being ripped opened like a piece of meat. I started to cry as he continued to enter me over and over again, but something didn't feel right. I know every man's dick is different, and I've only had Dagger inside of me, but something about this dick wasn't right.

As I laid there doing nothing, I heard my father's voice screaming at me, telling me to fight. With as much strength I could muster up, I grabbed for his face, attempting to claw through the mask, but with my wrist tied together, there wasn't much I could do.

"You know, the more you fight back, the worse it's going to be for you right," he said, grabbing a hand full of my hair and slamming my head against the floor of the van. It made a thud sound as my head connected with the floor.

I was already dizzy before this, but this just made it worst. My scream as well as his heavy breathing, went silent. Not because I had stopped, but because the hit to my head somehow knocked my damn hearing out. I tried to lift my head, but it felt heavy. My body felt like it was ready to give up on me. I don't know if it was from how hard my head had hit against the floor, or from the many glasses of champagne that I had.

"My husband will make you pay for this," I managed to say.

"Fuck Dagger and fuck you. This is the universe making the two of you pay for fucking over family. Nobody wins when the family feuds," was the last thing I heard before I was hit in the face with something and I passed out.

To Be Continued...

OTHER RELEASES FROM MYIESHA

A New Jersey Love Story 1-4
Knight in Chrome Armor: 1-3
Disturbed: An Unbalanced Love 1-3
He's Nothing Like Them Other Ones 1-3
Stealing His Heart: A Reckless Love 1-2
Pistol and Zynovia: She Fell in Love with a Boss 1-3
Sincerely Yours, A Savage 1-3
Bouquets & Berettas 1-2
A New Jersey Love Story: Heirs to the Throne

ABOUT THE AUTHOR

Thank you so much for your support
With Love,
Myiesha S. Mason

facebook.com/AuthorMyiesha
instagram.com/_miss_mason

UNTITLED

Be sure to LIKE our Major Key Publishing page on Facebook!

CPSIA information can be obtained
at www.ICGtesting.com
Printed in the USA
LVHW04s2117090818
586500LV00014B/1047/P